Walter S. Landor, Stephen Wheeler

Letters and other Unpublished Writings of Walter Savage Landor

Walter S. Landor, Stephen Wheeler

Letters and other Unpublished Writings of Walter Savage Landor

ISBN/EAN: 9783337391287

Printed in Europe, USA, Canada, Australia, Japan

Cover: Foto ©Andreas Hilbeck / pixelio.de

More available books at **www.hansebooks.com**

LETTERS

AND OTHER

UNPUBLISHED WRITINGS

OF

WALTER SAVAGE LANDOR

EDITED BY

STEPHEN WHEELER

WITH PORTRAITS

LONDON

RICHARD BENTLEY AND SON

Publishers in Ordinary to Her Majesty the Queen

1897

PREFACE

LANDOR makes Boccaccio say, concerning the critic, that he walks in a garden which is not his own, and must neither pluck the flowers to embellish his discourse, nor break off branches to display his strength. Lying about Landor's garden were a few withered sprays and faded leaves. They are here collected, not with a critical design, but rather for a memorial. All who take interest in Landor's writings or in his life will surely prize them; while for others, perhaps they might help to shape a conception of his character and quality not far removed from the truth.

Landor was never more himself than when writing to intimate friends, and a number of his letters will be found here. Some day it may be thought right to publish a larger selection from his correspondence. Beside what is now given, there is a quantity of verse hitherto unprinted; together with compositions in prose which might otherwise have been lost beyond recall. Lastly, certain bibliographical notes are appended, in the hope that they may be of some assistance to inquirers in this side-path of literary exploration. One work of Landor's —'Letters of a Canadian'—traces of which are now discovered, seems to have been altogether unknown to his editors and biographers.

In Chapter V., where something is said about Landor's 'Poems from the Arabic and Persian,' there is a reference to an Arabic poet, Fazil Beg, described as the grandson of Sheikh Dahir of Acre. Mr. Ellis, of the British Museum, has kindly enlightened my ignorance of this author and his works, which, however, are more curious than edifying. According to J. von Hammer-Purgstall and Mr. E. J. W. Gibb, Fazil Beg was a son, not a grandson, of the ruler of Acre (Tahir Pasha, the name should be); but whereas Volney states that only one of Tahir's sons was spared by Hassan Pasha, Mr. Gibb tells us that Fazil Beg had a younger brother, Kiamil Beg, who was also spared and taken to Constantinople, and that this Kiamil

Beg was likewise a poet. A Turkish poem, by Fazil Beg— the *Zenan Nama*, or 'Book of Women'—has within late years been translated into French. It bears no resemblance to Landor's supposed translations, and their original must be sought for either in Fazil Beg's Arabic poems or in his brother's.

To Lady Graves-Sawle and Dr. Arthur de Noé Walker my warmest thanks are due. To Mr. Stephen Luke, C.I.E., I am indebted for photographs of the Hon. Rose Aylmer's tomb, the situation of which was first pointed out by Dr. Busteed, in his 'Echoes of Old Calcutta,' a singularly interesting volume of Anglo-Indian memories.

CONTENTS.

CHAPTER   PAGE

I. A DESK OF CEDAR-WOOD . . . I

II. IMAGINARY CONVERSATIONS AND PROSE

             FRAGMENTS 25

III. LOVES AND FRIENDSHIPS . . . 64

IV. SOME OLD LETTERS 93

V. FRAGMENTS IN PRINT 131

VI. LANDOR AND HIS CONTEMPORARIES . 152

VII. UNPUBLISHED VERSE . . . 184

BIBLIOGRAPHY 245

LIST OF ILLUSTRATIONS

PORTRAIT OF WALTER SAVAGE LANDOR, FROM A DRAW-
ING BY COUNT D'ORSAY   .   .   *Frontispiece*

ROSE AYLMER'S TOMB AT CALCUTTA, FROM A PHOTO-
GRAPH.   .   .   .   *To face page* 72

PORTRAIT OF IANTHE, FROM A MINIATURE FOUND IN
LANDOR'S DESK   .   .   .   *To face page* 76

PORTRAIT OF WALTER SAVAGE LANDOR, FROM A BUST
BY JOHN GIBSON, R.A..   .   *To face page* 244

WALTER SAVAGE LANDOR

CHAPTER I.

A DESK OF CEDAR-WOOD.

High on a hill a goodly Cedar grewe,
Of wondrous length and streight proportion,
That farre abroad her daintie odours threwe;
Mongst all the daughters of proud Libanon,
Her match in beauty was not anie one.'

ED. SPENSER.

MORE than half a century ago, a cedar-tree at Ipsley Court in Warwickshire, whether by wind or lightning, was shattered and overthrown. 'Surely about the root,' the owner of the estate wrote forthwith to his sister, 'there must be some pieces large enough to make a little box of. Pray keep them for me.' His desire had been foreseen; and not long after, on his seventieth birthday, his sister sent him a cedar-wood writing-desk.   Battered somewhat, scarred with marks of toil and travel, that desk even now contains what to its first owner were relics above price.   For eighteen years it served the man for whom it was lovingly fashioned, Walter Savage Landor.   Another four-and-thirty years it remained in the hands of Landor's intimate friend, Arthur de Noé Walker. By Landor's friend it was given to me.

Landor once remarked that the scent of cedar produced a singular effect on him.   Even a cedar-pencil held unconsciously near his face would so absorb the senses that what he was about to write vanished altogether and irrecoverably.   Memory, alas ! may at times have played him false while he was sitting at this desk; more than once, what he called the ' latter-math of thought ' yielded a less goodly fragrance than a summer crop ; yet who will affirm that the desk of cedar-wood was to blame ?   Other, even less palpable influences were about that ' imperial brow.'   From the first hour he used it his steps were hastening to the river all must cross :

' Happy, who reach it ere they count the loss
  Of half their faculties and half their friends.'

It was no perfume born of Eastern wood-land and hillside — scattered, he once said, from the wings of angels as they lighted on cedars of Lebanon—that could overcloud his intellect or disturb his fancy, but rather the damps of life's autumn that 'sink into the leaves and prepare them for the necessity of their fall.' And if the words that came were not at all times the happiest and the best, if the verses were not always *carmina linenda cedro, et levi servanda cupresso,* if some small portion of prose and poetry thus written in these his declining years might more wisely have been blotted out, there is nothing to marvel at :

> ' Neither is Dirce clear,
> Nor is Ilissos full throughout the year.'

Yet we may not forbear to guard and preserve whatever can animate our memories of a great writer.

To return to the desk of cedar-wood. The tree out of which it was made was perhaps one of 'two solitary cedar twins,' at Ipsley Court, referred to in some unpublished verses, not otherwise remarkable, which I find in a letter of Landor's written when he lived in Florence in 1860; cedars—

> 'Fifty years old, and spreading wide
> O'er the soft glebe their hospitable arms.'

These same trees also inspired one of his published poems:

> 'Cypress and cedar! gracefullest of trees,
> Friends of my boyhood! ye, before the breeze,
> As lofty lords before an Eastern throne
> Bend the whole body, not the head alone.'

Everyone has heard of the countless cedars that Landor planted on his Welsh estate. He obtained thousands of cones from Lebanon, but the experiment in forestry turned out ill. It might have fared better, perhaps, had Landor taken a hint from John Evelyn and tried the Bermudas cedar, 'of all others the most excellent and odoriferous';* so likely, moreover, as Evelyn heard, to thrive in other countries that 'twas pity, he thought, but it should be universally cultivated. Landor's failure at Llanthony, we know, did not cure him of his affection for cedar-trees. He seems

* Mr. John Evelyn, at Sayes Court, to Mr. William London at Barbados, September 27, 1681.

to have kept some of the cones and to have planted one in his garden at Fiesole. This at least I gather from the Latin verses here printed for the first time :

CEDRUS INSERITUR.

'Gaudete, o flores ! quam clauserat arca novennem
    Inseritur læta libera cedrus humo.
Mox illa æstivâ nutrix vos proteget umbrâ,
    Forsitan atque aliam, me quoque si merear.'

So it is not difficult to understand how, in Landor's eyes, the writing-desk, made from the wood of his favourite tree, and given to him by his best-beloved sister, acquired a value far above the intrinsic worth of a roughly-shapen piece of furniture, the modest essay, one doubts not, of a village carpenter. He used it constantly, carried it with him on his hurried flight to Italy, and only parted with it, after eighteen years of close companionship, when he believed his end was approaching. Then it was that he wrote to the Contessa Geltrude Baldelli, the sister of his friend Arthur de Noé Walker, the letter that follows :

'DEAR COUNTESS,
    'In a little while I must make a long journey, and I shall not be able to take London on my way.

Therefor I keep my promise to Arthur in making a present to him of my writing-desk and its contents. During these several days, I have been almost entirely deaf and insensible, and have seen nobody but the kind and accomplisht Mr. Twisleton, brother of Lord Say and Seale. He comes to visit me almost every evening. Whenever you have an opportunity, or whenever Arthur comes to Florence, give him my desk. Meanwhile, believe me,

' Yours sincerely,
' W. S. LANDOR.

' May 15, '63.'

The Contessa forwarded the letter to her brother, writing herself on the same sheet of paper :

' Mr. Landor is apparently better than usual, but persuaded that he will not live many days. I have the desk in my keeping.'

With his habitual intolerance of delays, Landor would not quietly await a fitting occasion for sending the desk by a safe hand to London. A few days later he had it brought back to him, and himself arranged for its despatch. A postscript to a letter of his dated May 27, 1863, says :

'I trust the writing-case will have reached you. It contains the only valuables I possess—two miniatures—keep them for my sake as I kept them for theirs they represent. The *spedizionario* has promist me to pay the carriage to London.'

What the desk contained when it was opened and examined, more than thirty years afterwards, the following pages will in part discover. The task has not been undertaken without a certain trepidation. Landor himself was quick to resent the heartless effrontery that lays bare to idly inquisitive eyes the more sacred relics of the famous dead; while the *impedimenta* of great men—the chair that one author of repute sat in, the pen that another handled—would not, in his opinion, be worth a search. Still less would he have wished that every word he wrote himself should be redeemed from oblivion by the indiscriminating reverence of an after age. He warmly protested against 'the disinterment of the rankest garbage of Swift and Dryden,' who as it was, he considered, had left too much above ground; and the later successes of lettered curiosity-hunters would have excited his angry contempt. Nothing, therefore, either of the papers or of the little possessions which for some reason or other he had kept so many years will be longer preserved, save such as may help to a better comprehension of his life and writings.

I must explain that there was much more in the desk, when it was my privilege to examine its contents, than had been placed in its various compartments when Landor sent it to his friend in London. All that was originally there still remains — miniatures, an old pocket-book, a purse, a pen-wiper, some spectacles and eye-glasses that Landor had used, and other belongings, including one most precious relic, to be mentioned hereafter : few who love Landor's memory will hear of its existence without emotion. Along with these, Landor's friend kept many of the letters he had received from him ; and as their correspondence extended over the space of sixteen years, this portion of the treasure would make many a collector of autographs turn pale with envy. Moreover, Landor's friend had acted the part of inter-mediary—no easy function—between the exiled poet and a London publisher. Thus it fell out that the author's manuscript of a whole volume of his works came to be kept in the desk, together with many of his writings, which at one time or another he wished to have inserted in the last of his books, but which—either because he changed his mind, or for some other cause—were eventually held back. The manuscript of the 'Heroic Idyls' (London, 1863)—Landor's last work—has been deposited in the British Museum.

Then, again, there is a separate collection of prose and poetry, most of it in Landor's handwriting, the rest consisting of portions of his earlier books in print, but with his manuscript emendations. To this separate parcel a curious history is attached. Landor had heard, or read in some literary journal, that a publisher in the United States proposed to bring out a complete edition of his works. A volume of selections had already appeared there, and shortly before the outbreak of the Civil War Mr. Field of Boston made arrangements for bringing out a reprint of the two-volume edition of Landor's works published by Mr. Moxon in 1846. Landor had always hoped to be widely read beyond the Atlantic. 'I could never live there,' he said, 'because they have no cathedrals or painted glass'; yet he numbered many distinguished

Americans among his friends—Emerson the philosopher, Story the sculptor and poet, Mr. James Russell Lowell, diplomatist and man of letters, and many more. For upwards of half a century he had taken a keen interest in American politics. His first volume of imaginary conversations was dedicated in 1824 to ' Major-General Stopford, Adjutant-General in the army of Columbia,' and a connection of his own by marriage; for the handsome ex-Guardsman, who had renounced the gaieties of London to serve under Bolivar, had married Mrs. Landor's sister. A subsequent volume was dedicated to Bolivar himself. George Washington and Benjamin Franklin, as well as the founder of Pennsylvania, figure in Landor's dialogues; and he would frequently put his own speculations on American affairs into the mouths of European potentates and statesmen. When he learnt, therefore, that his writings were about to be laid before American readers in a becoming shape, he was profoundly gratified. No pains must be spared to make the edition perfect. Packet after packet of corrections and additions was sent to Boston from Via Nunziatina, Florence, where Landor spent his last years on earth.

'Nothing in the course of my long life ever went on smoothly.' So he wrote to his friend in London early in 1861, and in the same letter he referred to the manuscripts sent to Mr. Field of Boston, who was to have begun the printing of the American edition at this very time. 'It is probable,' he added, 'that recent occurrences in America will divert the public attention from literature.' And so it was. Mr. Field presently wrote to say that the approaching struggle between North and South compelled him to postpone the publication of an American edition; whereupon, at Landor's request, the manuscripts were sent to the same friend in London who had undertaken to see the 'Heroic Idyls' through the press. By him they were presently put away in the cedar-wood desk, where the other day I found them, along with the rest of a veritable treasure trove.

But I must leave to others the task of appraising the value of what is thus brought to light—prose and poetry, letters to ·friends, emendations of what was already in print, suggestions for new editions, and the little drawer full of keepsakes from people known and unknown. Not being an expert in such computation, I would say the lot together is worth an old song, provided Landor's comment on the contrary phrase be borne in remembrance: ' We often hear that such or such a thing is not worth an old song. Alas! how very few things are.'

Mr. Forster, when he prepared his eight-volume edition of Landor's life and works, either was not aware of the existence of these papers, or did not trouble his head about them. An accident, which I for one sincerely deplore, concealed them from Mr. Sidney Colvin's knowledge when he was writing those two most delightful volumes which have done more than all Mr. Forster's cumbrous efforts to convince Englishmen that Landor is among the immortals. They were equally inaccessible to Landor's latest editor, Mr. Crump. But if ever there is to be a final and complete edition of the imaginary conversations, miscellaneous prose works, and poems of the great writer whose first book was published when Byron was a schoolboy, whose last appeared when some of the best known writers of to-day had already bound themselves to the idle trade of versifying, this collection—as I think the account here given of it will abundantly prove—cannot possibly be overlooked. Not that every scrap of paper Landor wrote on, every last leaf that fell from the old tree, need be handed down to posterity. Some of these sweepings from his study—to use one of the titles he thought of for a projected volume of miscellanies—might be swept into the sea without detriment, even with positive advantage, to his fame. Others, again, he had himself rejected on second thoughts, and when his second thoughts were the best; for quick as he often was to demolish a friendly objection, if it was an unfounded one, he could also acquiesce when he found that a flaw invisible to his own eyes was patent to others. The composition so condemned would be put aside without a word. This is the explanation of many of the alterations noted in Mr. Crump's *variorum* edition of his works; and I have reason to know that a few, at any rate, of the fragments in his desk were withheld from the printer by his own wish and from the same motives. His wishes, need I say, as far as they can be discerned, shall be respected.

Besides manuscripts and printed papers and

the more interesting relics which will be mentioned presently, Landor's desk contained a few odds and ends either of smaller account or less easy to identify. There is an old-fashioned purse, a network of silk with gilt rings and tassels, such as our grandmothers were wont to use when they wore their best gowns. No doubt there is a story to it, if one knew. Mrs. Dashwood* once gave Landor a purse, together with some lady-like verses on the presentation, to which Landor responded:

> ' I should think it a sin
> Any *paul* to put in
> A net that the Graces have woven ;
> And if ever I do 't
> May he kick me whose foot
> (They say who have seen it) is cloven.'

The verses may be found in Ablett's ' Literary Hours,' and their authorship is avowed in a manuscript note in the South Kensington copy of that rare volume. Mrs. Dashwood's purse, however, was of a bright crimson hue ; this one is blue and orange.

Nor do I know why Landor kept the silk

---

* Daughter of Dean Shipley and cousin to Francis Hare.

watch-guards and eye-glass cords, though among the papers there are verses to Miss Edith Story, the daughter of the accomplished American sculptor, thanking her for some such gift :

   ' With pride I wear a silken twine,
   Precious as every gift of thine ;
   Only less precious than the chain
   For which so many sigh in vain.'*

Three pairs of spectacles and a double eye-glass, with rims of tortoiseshell, were perhaps bought by Landor for himself. He once told Words-worth that thinking ruined one's eyesight more surely than reading, and that those who read much and think little do not suffer. There is also a double eye-glass in silver and tortoise-shell of a more antiquated pattern. A French lady gave Landor some eye-glasses that once belonged to Talleyrand, but by Landor they were given to Sir Henry Bulwer.

A quantity of flower seeds sent to Landor, I fancy, by his sister from Ipsley Court, some pieces of ribbon, linked coat-buttons, a pocket-book with one or two almost illegible entries, in which one can make out little else except the

* Landor MSS.

name of Kossuth, an unrecognized photograph, and a penwiper may also be mentioned here. Of other relics the reader shall hear in due course.

But before describing the more noteworthy contents of the desk of cedar-wood, a word should be said of the circumstances that have made me its custodian. Though Landor's writings first found a place among my most intimate books years ago in India, it was some little time before I became aware of his Indian associations. Even when I lodged in Russell Street, Calcutta, I did not know that Rose Aylmer's uncle gave his name to the street, and that she died in that very quarter of the City of Palaces; nor when I called with letters of introduction on the distinguished officer who held the post of Surveyor-General had I any notion that he was Landor's brother-in-law and god-son. In course of time I discovered that some of Landor's dearest friends had been in India; and I often wondered then who it was he had addressed in the lines:

'After hot days in the wild wastes of war,
    Where India saw thy sword shine bright above
    The helms of thousand brave.'

At length a happy chance made me acquainted with Dr. Arthur de Noé Walker, late Captain in the Madras Army, the very man for whom these verses were written; and I discovered that Dr. Walker had been Landor's friend for thirty years. But for his unfailing kindness and sympathy these chapters would not be written. Besides placing the papers in Landor's desk at my disposal, he has helped me more than I can tell to a better knowledge of his old friend's life and character. I have to thank him, too, for what is perhaps the best of the portraits of Landor here reproduced.

What Dr. Walker thinks of the various likenesses, pictures, photographs, and engravings, which we have looked at together, merits of course particular attention. Writing to him from Florence in February 23, 1860, Landor said :

' You shall certainly have a photograph of me, altho' I refused to allow Forster, who edited the two volumes of my works, to place an engraving before them. I utterly detest thrusting my head into people's faces, with *here I am*. In former days no fewer than thirteen portraits of me have been taken—most of them miniatures. Fisher painted three, Bewick three, and Boxall two.'

Of these thirteen portraits I can only find trace of eight, not counting engravings, photographs, and copies. In 1804, when Landor was in his thirtieth year, and was living in somewhat profuse style at Bath, Nathaniel Dance, R.A.,* painted his portrait. An engraving forms the frontispiece to the first edition of Forster's 'Biography' of Landor, vol. i.; but it was omitted in subsequent editions. Of this portrait Forster wrote: 'The eye is fine, but black hair covers all the forehead, and you recognize the face of the later time quite without its fulness, power, and animation. The stubbornness is there, without the softness; the self-will untamed by any experience; plenty of energy, but a want of emotion.' The late Lord Houghton, who knew Landor intimately, and understood him better than Mr. Forster could, found no trace in this portrait of the sweetness and humour about the mouth which redeemed 'the anti-social' character of the upper features. Still, it may serve to convey some idea of what Landor was like at

* Afterwards Sir Nathaniel Dance Holland, Bart., who died in 1811. Many of his portraits pass for the work of Sir Joshua Reynolds.

this early stage of his life. It portrays a man conscious of great powers, who has not yet found his opportunity for exerting them.

In the British Museum there is a portrait of Landor by William Bewick, 'done at Florence, September 12, 1826.' He was then in his fifty-second year, and had published two editions of the first series of 'Imaginary Conversations.' The hair no longer hangs in curls over his forehead, which is now bald, but the lips close firmly, and the eyes show a fixed resolution. In the year following a bust of Landor was modelled by Gibson. Writing to his sister Elizabeth on April 25, 1828, Landor said :

'Gibson came to me the very day Ackleton brought me Robert's poem,* and I gave him two sittings, one in the morning and one in the evening. There have been three days, and there will be four more, before he takes the cast in plaster of paris. I am told that Chantrey is equal to him in busts, but very inferior in genius. The one is English upon principle, the other Attic.'

Landor thought highly of Gibson. He makes Alfieri say of him and Thorwaldsen : 'I have seen no drawings, not even Raphael's, more

* 'The Impious Feast,' by Robert Eyres Landor.

pure and intellectual than theirs. I suspect their native countries will never be competent to form a just estimate of their merit. We may say of each, *utinam noster esses*.' Yet for all that, the bust of Gibson, who often failed in portraiture, is considered by Dr. Walker to be anything but a good likeness; and the photograph from it (now reproduced) need only be studied for the less minute proportions it records. It was made in marble for that 'Lord of the Celtic dells,' Mr. Joseph Ablett, and the photograph was given me by Landor's brother-in-law, General Sir Henry Landor Thuillier.

But I should like here to refer to another portrait of Landor at this time—a portrait neither in marble nor on canvas. The Countess of Blessington first met Landor at Florence in June, 1827, and her impressions were recorded in that vivacious book of travel, 'The Idler in Italy':

'There is a natural dignity which appertains to him, that suits perfectly with the style of his conversation and his general appearance. His head is one of the most intellectual ones imaginable, and would serve as a good illustration in support of the theories of Phrenologists. The forehead broad and prominent; the mental organs largely developed; the eyes quick and intelligent, and the mouth full of benevolence.'

The next portrait, in another medium than words, is a lithograph from a pencil drawing by the Countess of Blessington's friend, Count Alfred D'Orsay. The original, Mr. Colvin says, was done in 1825. In the autumn Landor paid a long visit to Mr. Ablett at Llanbedr; and when two years afterwards Mr. Ablett, in memory of the occasion, printed 'Literary Hours by various Friends,' a lithograph from D'Orsay's pencil sketch was used as a frontispiece. 'Corrected from D'Orsay's, in which the chin was much too low and too much head behind.' That was Landor's own comment, written by himself in the copy of 'Literary Hours' at South Kensington Museum. But even with these corrections the likeness can hardly be regarded as a pleasing one. It seems to lay stress on what was least lovable in Landor's expression. In 1839, however, Count D'Orsay drew, most likely on the stone, a more finished portrait, which even those who never saw the original would at once pronounce to be a better likeness than the earlier sketch. Indeed, Dr. Walker, who gave me his copy of the print, thinks it not only very like Landor, but one of the very few portraits extant that are like him. Landor was now sixty-four, and had been living for more than a year at Bath, whence he paid frequent visits to London, being ever a welcome guest at Gore House, under whose hospitable roof, as he says somewhere, ' a greater number of remarkable men assembled from all nations than under any other, since roofs took the place of caverns.'

A little before the date of Count D'Orsay's second portrait, Landor gave sittings to Mr. William Fisher, a young artist who was presently to become a Royal Academician. To Mr. Fisher, Landor addressed the well-known lines beginning :

'Conceal not Time's misdeeds, but on my brow
        Retrace his mark ;
  Let the retiring hair be silvery now
        That once was dark :
  Eyes that reflected images too bright
        Let clouds o'ercast,
  And from the tablet be abolisht quite
        The cheerful past.'

Southey admired this portrait, but Landor

said the colour was too like a dragon's belly. The original was the prcperty of Mr. Kenyon, by whose residuary legatees it was given to Crabbe Robinson,* who in turn bequeathed it to the National Portrait Gallery. An en- graving on wood from this portrait was pub- lished in the *Century Magazine* for February, 1888, in which there also appeared an article on Landor by Mr. James Russell Lowell, followed by some letters of Landor's to Miss Mary Boyle. Another and, I think, a better portrait by the same artist is in the possession of Lady Graves-Sawle.

In 1852 Mr., afterwards Sir, William Boxall painted Landor's portrait. An engraving on steel from this picture is given in the second volume of Mr. Forster's 'Biography' (first edition 1869). Landor himself considered it an excellent likeness, as may be seen from his letter to Forster written in. December, 1852 :

' Perhaps when I am in the grave, curiosity may be excited to know what kind of countenance that creature had who imitated nobody, and whom nobody imitated : the man who walked thro' the

---

* H. Crabbe Robinson's Diary, ii. 360.

crowd of poets and prose-men and never was toucht by anyone's skirts : who walked up to the ancients and talked with them familiarly, but never took a sup of wine or a crust of bread in their houses. If this should happen, and it probably will within your lifetime, then let the good people see the old man's head by Boxall.'*

Yet, as Mr. Colvin remarks, there is much that was uncharacteristic and somewhat feebly benignant in Boxall's portrait. It is now in the South Kensington Museum.

A striking portrait of Landor, apparently from a photograph, may be found in the fourth volume of Mr. Crump's edition of his works. It was taken a year after the date of Fisher's portrait, to which, however, it bears very little resemblance, being much more like the photograph prefixed to the second volume of Mr. Forster's edition, said to have been taken in 1849. Both these portraits are declared by Dr. Walker to be excellent, though it must be added that they only represent Landor in a particular mood. His expression would change in an instant to one of keen animation and the most genial kindness.

* This letter was omitted in subsequent editions.

CHAPTER II.

IMAGINARY CONVERSATIONS AND PROSE FRAGMENTS.

' I seek not many, many seek me not.'
W. S. LANDOR.

COULD Landor himself be consulted as to which of the papers in his desk he desired more especially to be given to the world, he would doubtless say: Print the imaginary conversations. Of these there are three hitherto unpublished, or, at any rate, not to be found in the collected editions of his works; one being a ' dramatic scene ' in verse, which was at first written as a prose dialogue. All three were sent by Landor to Boston, to be included in an American edition of his prose and poetry; and the subsequent fate of the parcel has already been told.

By far the finest of the newly-discovered

conversations is that in which Frà Girolamo or Jeronimo Savonarola, preacher and martyr, learns that he has been sentenced to death, vindicates his past conduct, and speaks of the end that awaits him with fortitude and composure. George Eliot, in a historic novel, and Mr. Alfred Austin, in a dramatic poem, have drawn more elaborate and finished pictures of Savonarola; and there is not enough in this brief scene to permit a comparison between their treatment of the subject and Landor's. But the conversation, written though it was in its author's eighty-sixth year, is wanting neither in vividness of imagination nor in eloquence. The Republican Friar* who had so courageously defied the Borghia and the Medici, who had defended liberty and religion against the flagrant scandals of the Papacy and the corroding decadence that hung like a plague-cloud over Florence; the man of suffering who had passed through the torment of the rack, and for whom the pains of death were made ready as he conversed, appears only for a few moments on Landor's stage, but in those few moments a life's tragedy is concentrated.

* 'Savonarola and his Times,' by Professor Villari.

Historical accuracy must not be sought for. If a true account is wanted of Savonarola's last days, we must go elsewhere. The whole story has been carefully reconstructed by Professor Villari. The martyrdom of Savonarola and the two monks, Domenicho of Padua and Silvestro Marufi, took place on the morning of May 23, 1498. On April 8 (Palm Sunday), Savonarola had surrendered to his enemies. Since then he had been brought for trial first before the judges appointed by the Signory of Florence, and afterwards before the Ecclesiastical Commissioners sent by the Pope; and for upwards of a month he had repeatedly undergone long and grievous tortures. When not in the presence of his judges, he was confined in the Alberghettino, a small chamber in the tower of the Palazzo Vecchio, where it must be supposed that this conversation takes place. The sentence of the Pope's Commissioners was pronounced on May 22, and was made known to Savonarola the same evening. The next morning it was carried out. The three Friars were hanged, and their bodies then committed to the flames. Professor Villari does not name the messengers who informed Savonarola of the punishment to be inflicted on him, but says that they found him kneeling in prayer. 'On hearing the fatal announcement he expressed neither grief nor joy, but continued his devotions with increased fervour.' Between that time and the hour when he was led out to execution he saw and spoke with Jacopo Niccolini, member of a benevolent society, with a Benedictine friar who came to receive his last confession, and with his two companions in misfortune, whom he was allowed to meet on the night of May 22, and again on the morrow when he partook of the Sacrament with them.

There was no opportunity for such a conversation as Landor imagines, unless, indeed, we suppose that Savonarola was speaking, not to the Prior of San Marco,* but to Jacopo Niccolini, to whom he foretold the calamities that were to fall on Florence, adding, 'Bear well in mind that these things will come to pass when there shall be a Pope named Clement.' That the three monks died, not in the flames,

* Professor Villari does not say who had succeeded Savonarola as Prior of San Marco ; nor, indeed, does he say that a successor had been elected.

but by the hangman's rope, has already been stated. Landor may have been misled on this point by Sismondi.

It was in the latter half of the year 1860 that Landor wrote and published an imaginary conversation in Italian—' Savonarola e il Priore di San Marco.' It formed a small octavo pamphlet of seven pages; and the proceeds of the sale were to be given for the relief of Garibaldi's wounded followers.* That hero's victories over the Neapolitan troops in Sicily had roused all Landor's enthusiasm. Verses were written by him, both English and Latin, in Garibaldi's honour; and the little cottage at Siena, where Landor was now staying, must have rung with revolutionary sentiment and loud denunciation of ' Gallia's basest brood.' Before the end of the year he also completed this English translation of the dialogue, and despatched it to Mr. Field, the Boston publisher, to whom he had already sent the original version in Italian. On the back of the paper containing the translation he has written :

* The approximate date may be inferred from Landor's own letters, and from the fact that Garibaldi set sail for Sicily from Genoa on May 5, 1860.

' My dear Sir,

'In the Italian dialogue I sent to you much was omitted by the printer's fear that the sentiments would offend the higher powers and obstruct the publication. It gave me some trouble to compose, and I was urged to give the whole in English, which I now send. . . . With respectful compliments, and wishing you a happy new year, I remain, my dear sir,

'Very truly yours,

'W. S. Landor.'

The few words omitted refer to a correction which Landor hoped the American printers would make in one of his earlier compositions. I will now give the conversation :

SAVONAROLA AND THE PRIOR OF S. MARCO.

Prior.

Jeronimo! dear Jeronimo! oftentimes have I been afflicted, but never so grievously as in this hour. Thou art abandoned to thy enemies, and there is no escape. The Holy Father* has found thee guilty.

Savonarola.

Alas! how many has he found guilty, and how many has he made so! *My* Holy Father, the

---

* Pope Alexander VI. (Roderigo Borghia).

Father who is in heaven, has too often found me guilty, even from infancy. Nevertheless has He deigned to show me the light of His countenance, and to confer on me the office of proclaiming His will. And now His right hand guides me on the road to expiate my many sins.

PRIOR.

Thy many sins? What mortal ever lived more chastely, more charitably, more devoutly? And to die so! Oh, God of mercy! can human flesh endure the surrounding flames?

SAVONAROLA.

Yes; that flesh which God hath prepared for it.

PRIOR.

The Church has been openly offended. Why?

SAVONAROLA.

Because the Church opposed God openly. Tell me, have I ever uttered a word contrary to the doctrine of the Apostols? Frequently have I preached before the people, but have abstained from declaring this truth, that under the seat of our Roman pontifs more Christian blood has been shed on behalf of Europe than under all the worst Roman emperors in the whole of it.

PRIOR.

It may be true; but there always is danger in speaking ill of dignitaries.

SAVONAROLA.

If I understand the word, it means the *worthy*. Before them I stand humiliated, not before the arrogant and presumptuous.

I am condemned to death; so art thou, so are all, even ere they cried from the cradle.

PRIOR.

Imperturbable is thy faith, thy courage super-human.

SAVONAROLA.

Superhuman it is, but it is not mine. I have followed with tardy pace the Precursor. He who walks in the dark will be guided more safely by one large and clear light, although distant, than by many smaller which sparkle on both sides of him. The Apostols have directed me, and my support was Christ.

PRIOR.

Yet the first and most sublime of martyrs, our Saviour himself, prayed of his Father that the bitter cup might pass from him.

SAVONAROLA.

It did not pass from him. The Son drank of it, bowed his head and died. Better men than I am have borne testimony to the truth; I also have been deemed worthy to die for it.

PRIOR.

Better men! None, none.

SAVONAROLA.

Say not so. It appears to have been the will of Providence that some of them should live longer and teach more effectually. The fruit in the garden of Bethlehem will ripen in its season. Enervated as are our Florentines, they will rise and stand firm and upright. Wicked princes, and pontifs wickeder still, have led them astray, corrupted and subjugated them; strangers, in conflict one with another, have trodden them down; liberators, as they called themselves and were believed, chained and sold them.

PRIOR.

We have lived to see this in our own days. We must pray for them.

SAVONAROLA.

Ye must, but others must rise from their knees. Such is the will of God: the Merciful is the Avenger.

PRIOR.

We men of peace should be silent.

SAVONAROLA.

Not when God commands us to speak and cry aloud. The Pontif is a puppet in the hands of France, brought out and shut up again at her will and pleasure. There is no vision to our eyes of an emperor like Henry of Luxemburg. Dante Alighieri, Petrarcha, Boccaccio, were not only nightingales that sang in the dark—which all three did—but they were prophetic, and intelligible to the attentive ear. The *Divina Commedia* should rather be entitled the *Divina Satira*. It has the fire of Phlegethon, and the bitterness of Styx.

What France ever was, she will ever be ; a slave the seller of slaves. Such have been lauded *in excelsis*. The wolf has degenerated into a fox, an animal by nature of shriller cry, yet approaching the sheepfold more cautiously. There was a time when princes on horseback chased this animal ; now they invest him with a golden collar, and domesticate him.

PRIOR.

Beware ! beware !

SAVONAROLA.

Truth, it appears, is a virgin too pure to be embraced. Whatever most interests her seems most reprovable. Yet the more free our thoughts are, the nearer are they to that region where Truth resides. Certainly it is not in the Maremma Romana. God has taught me his holy Word, and has commanded me also to teach it.

PRIOR.

They who find a jewel do not prudently and safely wear it in all places.

SAVONAROLA.

We have found what is richer than a jewel, we have found what constitutes the bread of life. The wheat that nourishes nations was but a grain at first : many crops sprang from it, many were mildewed, many trodden underfoot, as we have seen and see now, yet the seed is incorruptible, and will endure for ever. Italy will not always be what Italy is now. The most acute of men will reason and reflect, and will drive away those who forbid it. What Christ has forbidden they will call to mind, and act accordingly. He forbade even his disciples to call him Lord. The impostor who calls himself, and orders others to call him *His Holiness, His Beatitude, God's Vicegerent*, etc., offends against God's express commandment.

PRIOR.

Be cool, my brother.

SAVONAROLA.

Presently I shall be, if anything be left of me after this day's festival, celebrated with Druidical rites.

PRIOR.

That smile strikes into my inmost heart. Let us think rather of our Florentines. Let us hope for *them*, at least. Sound bodies may recover from heavy wounds, unsound succumb under lighter. If our Florentines are naturally brave, how greatly more brave will they become when they are virtuous. The corruption of a prince drops down on the heads and into the bosoms of

a people.   It is unsafe to animadvert on the living :
we may look back on Lorenzo de Medici, dead
recently.*   The defunct do not bite, and censure
falls without weight upon the sepulchre.

SAVONAROLA.

When I was called to the bedside of that dying
man, in order to hear his confession, according to
the wish he had exprest, not a single one of his
iniquities would he confess, nor any retribution
would he offer of what he had taken from his
country. '*First*,' said I, '*restore to the people the
liberty of which you deprived their fathers*.'   He turned
heavily round and disdainfully.   I was silent, and
left him.

PRIOR.

Peace to his soul ! if peace there can be where
such souls are.   Why could he not have been
contented in the station to which his fortune and
his genius had raised him ?   No other sovran in
Europe possessed such rich and extensive lands.
He could enjoy every climate in this little Tuscany.
In Pisa there is no severity of winter, in Pratolino
there is no oppressive heat.   The breezes of the
sea and of the Apennines were at his command.
Here in Florence he had the familiar society of the

---

* Lorenzo the Magnificent died in 1492.   His
interview with Savonarola should be read in Mr.
Alfred Austin's poem.

learned and philosophic, and poets sat convivially at his table.*

SAVONAROLA.

These maggots accelerated his corruption.

PRIOR.

The constitution of the poetic mind is naturally febrile, and is corroded in most by the chronic disease of jealousy. Lorenzo was subject to neither of these infirmities, not recognizing a rival in creatures so base. Adulation, if ever pardonable, is most so in poets. On Parnassus there are more flowers than fruits, the pasture is insufficient, and the air gives a keen appetite. The birds below perch on thorns, and when they alight they battle for a grain of millet. Not only poets, but persons in appearance more serious, consorted with Lorenzo: they might have taught him better.

SAVONAROLA.

They should have learnt better first. They spent days and nights in trivial, futile discussions, which they called Platonic.†

---

* Lorenzo de Medici 'encouraged all the worst tendencies of the age, and multiplied its corruptions. . . . During his reign, Florence was a continuous scene of revelry and dissipation.'—*Villari.*

† For an account of the disputes between the Platonic and Aristotelian schools, see Professor Villari. Savonarola wrote a compendium of both philosophies.

PRIOR.

Not improperly. The dialogues of Plato are mostly of no utility, for religion, morality, the sciences or the arts. They resemble the *pallone* with which our youthful citizens divert themselves, empty, turgid, round, weightless, thrown up into the air by one player, to be caught by another as it falls to the ground, and beaten back, bouncing, and covered with dust. In all his dialogues there is not a single one which impresses on the heart a virtuous or a tender sentiment, none of charity, none of philanthropy, none of patriotism.

SAVONAROLA.

Oh, the littleness of such a philosophy! We Christians know the true; we know where to find it; we know where sits the teacher. It is better to be guided thro' thorns than to sit idly with chatterers.

PRIOR.

It is well to ponder, but why pause now? And not very seriously.

SAVONAROLA.

I was reminded by your observations and similitudes of another pastime, in which a girl lays her hand down flat, another claps hers upon it, and thus rapidly and alternately, until both are tired of it, and one gives a slap on the knuckles of her playfellow and runs off laughing.

PRIOR.

Nothing discomposes my Jeronimo; I never found him so near to facetiousness before.

SAVONAROLA.

I look more willingly at tricks played in petticoats than under beards. Let them only be such as these.

Do not rise to go yet, my kind father! What is there to see below?

PRIOR.

Florence lies in bustle and confusion under the window: the sight makes me sorrowful.

SAVONAROLA.

Courage, courage, my Prior! The Sun of Righteousness will shine again. The Prophets will show their countenances thro' the clouds, and make their voices heard. Dante Alighieri lies in his tomb at Ravenna, but his spirit will return to our city and reanimate a half-dead people. Italy is not always to be sown with lies and irrigated with blood. Her sons are to be aware that the wine of the Last Supper is not drugged, is neither stimulant nor narcotic.

PRIOR.

What noise is that I hear? Whither are coming those four carts? With what are they laden?

SAVONAROLA.

I will tell thee.

PRIOR.

But why dost thou also rise from thy chair?

SAVONAROLA.

Those carts are laden with faggots and stakes; one of the stoutest is several ells long. What a number of poor starving creatures might be comforted at Christmas by such a quantity of materials.

The people are impatient for their bonfire, and the priests for their dinner.

PRIOR.

Embrace me, embrace me; sanctify a sinner. Jeronimo! shall we meet no more!

SAVONAROLA.

Thou knowest that meet we shall; God alone knows when. The days of man are numbered: there is no room for another numeral to mine; the punctuation of a period is enough. My future is beginning in this piazza; I can yet look beyond it. The Florentines will soon forget me; already they have forgotten themselves. Oblivion soon comes over cities; memory rests longer on a few faithful hearts. I and my words may pass away, but never will God's, however now neglected.

May thy years be as many as thy virtues, and as the benedictions on thy venerable head.

Turn not again, as thou seemest about to do, toward that window. When the smoke has been carried off by the wind, and the clouds are dissipated, then return to San Marco.

———

Landor sent another prose conversation to Mr. Field; and the scene of this, too, was laid in Italy. It is between the Countess of Albany, the widow of the Young Pretender, and her lover, Alfieri. When Landor was a young man, he once met the great Italian writer in a London book-shop, where he himself, oddly enough, was ordering copies of Alfieri's works. They were introduced; and Landor imparted his views on the French Revolution. 'Sir,' said Alfieri, 'you are a very young man; you are yet to learn that nothing good ever came out of France, or ever will.' Landor never forgot the meeting; and he used to say, long afterwards, that Alfieri was the man of all others with whom he himself was most nearly in agreement.

Alfieri appears in two of Landor's published conversations. The latest of these was printed in 1856, and was warmly praised by Thomas Carlyle. 'Do you think,' Carlyle asked Mr. Forster, ' the grand old Pagan wrote that piece just now ?   The sound of it is like the ring of Roman swords on the helmets of barbarians. An unsubduable old Roman !'   A hint was given in that conversation of the Countess of Albany's partiality for the French portrait-painter, M. Fabre, and of Alfieri's anger.   In the unpublished dialogue he tells the Countess that he will not be loved in fellowship with another :

COUNTESS.

A stranger might fancy you are jealous.   You know I receive all sorts of people at my *conversazioni*. Is there any stranger, any florid young Englishman, to whom you imagine I have taken a fancy ?   You know my taste better.   I hate assurance, I hate coarse flattery, I hate vulgarity.   On the score of politeness the English are clumsy originals and imperfect imitators.   You know I have a right to be their queen.

ALFIERI.

You have a right to be mine, and I never have forsworn my allegiance or transferred it.

COUNTESS.

Ah ! now you talk like an Italian, not like one of those rude islanders.

But a brief extract may suffice. To speak frankly, Landor in this conversation is dangerously near the commonplace, and it contains hardly a sentence or a sentiment that far inferior authors might not have written. The note he appends to it may be quoted, however. He writes :

' The Countess of Albany transferred her affections from Alfieri to one Fabre, a portrait-painter. Alfieri, stung with grief and indignation, left his rival long behind. On his deathbed the Countess sent a priest to administer the sacrament, who announced his errand. Alfieri turned round on his bed, and cried, *Who are you ?* On the priest's reply, he said, *I don't know you, and I don't want you, and I won't have you.* Poor soul ! He went off in a few hours, and without a wafer ! These facts were repeated to me thirty years ago by James Smith,[*] who heard them from Alfieri's physician, present in the chamber.

' W. S. L.'

I have found the same anecdote in a manuscript note, written by Landor in his copy of the magazine[†] containing the conversation

[*] James Smith, one of the authors of ' Rejected Addresses.'
[†] *Fraser's Magazine*, April, 1856.

between Alfieri and Metastasio. Here, after repeating what the poet said on his death-bed, Landor goes on to say of Alfieri :

'He was not the only wise man deluded by a weak and worthless woman. Love inflicted a curable wound, pride a mortal one. His monument is unworthy of Canova's hand. It exhibits a small portrait of the poet in *basso relievo*. Little is said of him, much of the Countess. Near it is the noblest monument in the whole church erected to Dante ; the sculpture by Nardi, with this brief inscription from the *Divina Commedia :* "Venerate l'altissimo poeta." '

The unpublished dramatic scene in blank verse, which was found with the others in Landor's desk, may be printed in full, and it needs but little in the way of introduction. In it he brings the Maid of Orleans, who had already appeared in one of his published conversations, before her judge, the Bishop of Beauvais.

JOAN OF ARC AND HER JUDGE.

JUDGE.

After due hearing in our court supreme
Of temporal and spiritual lords,
Condemn'd art thou to perish at the stake
By fire, forerunner of the flames below.
Hearest thou? Art thou stunn'd? Art thou gone
    mad?
Witch ! think not to escape and fly away,
As some the like of thee, 'tis said, have done.

JOAN.

The fire will aid my spirit to escape.

JUDGE.

Listen, ye lords. Her spirit ! Hear ye that?
She owns, then, to have her Familiar.
And whither (*to Joan*)—whither would the spirit,
    witch,
Bear thee ?

JOAN.
To Him who gave it.

JUDGE.
Lucifer ?
JOAN.

I never heard the name until thus taught.

JUDGE.
He hath his imps.

JOAN.

I see he hath.

JUDGE.

My lords!
Why look ye round, and upward at the rafters?
Smile not, infernal hag! for such thou art,
Altho' made comely to beguile the weak,
By thy enchantments and accursed spells.
Knowest thou not how many brave men fell
Under thy sword, and daily?

JOAN.

God knows best
How many fell—may their souls rest in peace!
We wanted not your land, why want ye ours?
France is our country, England yours; we hear
Her fields are fruitful: so were ours before
Invaders came and burnt our yellowing corn,
And slew the labouring oxen in the yoke,
And worried, in their pasture and their fold,
With thankless hounds, more sheep than were
　　devour'd.

JUDGE.

Thou wast a shepherdess. Were those sheep thine?

JOAN.

Whatever is my country's is mine too—
At least to watch and guard; I claim no more.
Ye drove the flocks adrift, and we the wolves.

JUDGE.

Thou shouldst have kept thy station in the field,
As ours do.

JOAN.

Nobles! have I not ?   Speak out.
In the field, too—the field ye shared with me—
The cause alone divided us.

JUDGE.

My lords !

Must we hear this from a peasant girl, a witch ?
Wolves we are call'd.   (*To Joan*) Do wolves, then,
    fight for glory ?

JOAN.

No; not so wicked, tho' by nature wild,
They seek their food, and, finding it, they rest.

JUDGE.

Sometimes the devil prompts to speak a truth
To cover lies, and to protect his brood.
But, *we* turn'd into wolves !—*we* Englishmen !
Tell us, thou knowing one, who knowest well—
Tell us, then, who are now the vanquishers.

JOAN.

They who will be the vanquished, and right soon.

JUDGE.

False prophets there have been, and thou art one,
And proud as he that sent thee here inspired.

Who ever saw thee bend before the high
And mighty men, the consecrate around—
They whom our Lord exalted, they who wear
The mitre on their brows ?

JOAN.

                    One—one alone—
Hath seen me bend, and may he soon more nigh,
Unworthy as I am !   I daily fall
Before the Man (for Man he would be call'd)
Who wore no mitre, but a crown of thorns
Wore he ; upon his hands no jewel'd ring,
But in the centre of them iron nails,
Half-hidden by the swollen flesh they pierced.

JUDGE.

Alert to play the pious here at last,
Thou scoffest Mother Church in these her sons,
Right reverend, worshipful, Beatitude's
Creation, Christ's and Peter's lawful heirs.

JOAN.

My mother Church enforced no sacrifice
Of human blood ; she never made flames drink it
Ere it boil over.   Dear were all *her* sons,
Nor unforgiven were the most perverse.

JUDGE.

Seest thou not here thy hearers sit aghast ?

JOAN.

Fear me not, nobles !   Ye were never wan
In battle ; ye were brave to meet the brave.
I come not now in helm or coat of mail,
But bound with cords, and helpless.   God incline
Your hearts to worthier service !

JUDGE.

                              Darest thou,
After such outrages on knight and baron,
To call on God, or name his holy name ?
'Tis mockery.

JOAN.

'Tis too often, not with me.
When first I heard his holy name I thought
He was my Father.   I was taught to call
My Saviour so, and both my parents did
The like, at rising and at setting sun
And when they shared the oaten cake at noon.

JUDGE.

So thou wouldst babble like an infant still ?

JOAN.

I would be silent, but ye bade me speak.

JUDGE.

Thou mayst yet pray—one hour is left for prayer.
Edify, then, the people in the street.

JOAN.

I never pray in crowds; our Saviour hears
When the heart speaks to him in solitude.
May we not imitate our blessed Lord,
Who went into the wilderness to pray?

JUDGE.

Who taught thee tales like this? They are forbidden.
Hast thou no supplication to the court?

JOAN.

I never sued in vain, and will not now.

JUDGE.

We have been patient ; we have heard thee prate
A whole hour by the bell ; we have endured
Impiety ; we have borne worse affronts.
My lords, ye have been bantered long enough.
The sorceress would have turned us into wolves,
And hunt us down ; she would be prophetess.

JOAN.

I am no sorceress, no prophetess ;
But this, O man in ermine, I foretell :
Thou and those round thee shall ere long receive
Your due reward. England shall rue the day
She entered France—her empire totters.

Pile

Ye sentinels, who guard those hundred heads

Against a shepherdess in bonds—pile high
The faggots round the stake that stands upright,
And roll the barrel gently down the street,
Lest the pitch burst the hoops, and mess the way.

(To the court).

Ye grant one hour ; it shall be well employed.
I will implore the pardon of our God
For you.   Already hath He heard my prayer
For the deliverers of their native land.

———

Landor also sent to America the 'Three Scenes, not for the Stage,' in which Diana of Poictiers, with the assistance of the Court Jester, obtains from the King, Francis I., a pardon for her father.   Mr. Forster, however, had a copy of this dramatic sketch, and printed it in his eight-volume edition.   The American version has, together with a few various readings, a characteristic note, in which Landor says : 'Francis and Henry IV. have always been the favorites of the French.   They were a couple of brave scoundrels at the best ; each of them would have been gibeted had he been a private man.'

A number of poems, long and short, found amongst Landor's manuscripts will be given in a later chapter, but there are some unpublished fragments in prose which it will be as well to deal with here. Many of them are mere jottings, though meant perhaps to be inserted in some conversation that was never written. Without a complete concordance one cannot indeed be absolutely certain that none of these fragments would be found, somewhere or other, in Landor's printed works; but I have done my best to avoid vain repetitions. Landor himself would occasionally say the same thing twice over. 'They who are afraid,' he wrote, 'of repeating what they have said before, may sometimes think they have spoken or written what they never have, and thus an animated being (such is a thought) is lost to the creation.' Here are some of these detached thoughts :

'We English are fond of quaffing diluted epigrams out of crystal cups, diamond-cut, reflecting and refracting.'

*   *   *   *   *

'It is usual with dogs to turn round before they lie down; so do gentlemen in the House of Commons.'

*   *   *   *   *

'Among the instances of absurd superlatives, I find in the "Aventure d'Amour of Dumas,' *Dents magnifiques.* Another, *nous avions passé une après-midi adorable.*'

It may be objected that *magnifique* and *adorable* are not, strictly speaking, superlatives; but Landor's meaning is clear enough.   He somewhere says that Italian prose-writers arc absurdly given to the use of superlatives, and styles the Italians the '*issimi* nation.'   In talking, he himself was not always over-careful to avoid the superlative of enthusiasm.   His brother, Robert Eyres Landor, relates that in the course of a morning's walk at Oxford they would pass a dozen strangers of the fairer sex, each one of whom Landor vowed was the most beautiful woman his eyes had ever rested on.

In another of these fragments Landor says:

'If I were askt what stanza or strophe I would rather have written than any other, I should doubt between Gray's " The boast of heraldry," etc., and George Herbert's

> '" Sweet day ! so cool, so calm, so bright,
>   The bridal of the earth and sky ;
> The dew shall weep thy fall to-night,
>   For thou must die."*

'If what couplet, I would go to the Latin, and stand again in doubt between that of Tibullus' *Te*

---

* The whole poem is quoted by Isaac Walton in his ' Compleat Angler.'

*teneam** and that of Johannes Secundus, *Non est suaviolum*, etc.'†

Landor has twice translated the verses from Tibullus :‡ once in his ' Citation of William Shakespeare,' and again in a little poem, ' On receiving a portrait,' which begins :

' To gaze on you when life's last gleams decline,
  And hold your hand, to the last clasp, in mine.'

Of the longer prose fragments the first is a retort to De Quincey's observations on Dr. Samuel Parr. Landor had been reading the essay on ' Whiggism in its Relation to Literature,'§ wherein De Quincey, after expressing a doubt whether one reader in three thousand would know who Dr. Parr was, went on to describe the friend of Landor's early days as a

* ' Te spectem, suprema mihi cum venerit hora
    Te teneam moriens deficiente manu.'
                                        TIBULLUS, I. i. 59.

† ' Non est suaviolum dare, lux mea, sed dare tantum
    Est desiderium flebile suavioli.'
                                        BASIUM, iii.

‡ Works, 1876, ii. 531, and viii. 77.

§ ' De Quincey's Works ' (1862), vol. v.

man whom it was impossible either to like or respect. He was a lisping slander-monger, De Quincey said—a retailer of gossip fitter for washerwomen over their tea than for scholars and statesmen. His reputation for learning was undeserved; his manners were unendurable. A boundless license of personal invective, an extravagance of brutality, an 'obstreperous laugh monstrously beyond the key of good society,' were also placed among the doctor's shortcomings. 'My object is,' wrote De Quincey, 'to value Dr. Parr's claims and to assign his true station both in literature and in other walks of life upon which he has come forward as a public man.' We are more insidious in our literary depreciations now-a-days; but De Quincey's method would have its advantages if one could trust his judgment and his honesty. Others had found much to like and even to love, in Dr. Parr's character. Robert Landor, though he admired Parr less than his brother did, pronounced De Quincey's attack to be grossly unfair. What Walter Landor thought of it may be seen from the following paper :

IN DEFENCE OF DR. PARR.

'Mr. de Quincey's attack on Parr is insolent and flippant, therefor admirably suited to a Review or Magazine or any popular publication. Parr had his foibles, as even the strongest men have. We never say of a weak one *he* has his foibles. Where *all* is weak they are unnoticed. Parr was incapable of a long continuous work, such as Hooker's was. His mind was *splintery*. But he seldom wrote a sentence without something good and striking in it. They are too often *tripartite*, as Johnson's are *bipartite*. His style is on no occasion to be imitated. For a style we must have recourse to Goldsmith, Blackstone, and the hated and persecuted Payne.* We need not go back to Addison, Swift, and Defoe.

'And here I am forced to remark what small hearts and twisted heads have some otherwise great men. Swift was the reviler of Defoe. I am grateful to Parr for much kindness and much instruction. He offered me the use of his library, but whenever I began to read a book, he would give it a running commentary. He wished me to write a history of England in Latin. This advice was injudicious. Few English names can be Latinized. The Dean of Westminster has lately desired me to write a Latin epitaph on Hallam; and Milnes made to me the same request in regard

---

* Thomas Paine, author of 'The Age of Reason.'

to his father. That of Milnes I declined at the time, but it soon occurred to me that Miln*es* has a Latin termination and declension. Miln*is* or Milnet*is*, and you have him in his toga.

'Now I return to Parr. I saw him in all his glory, when he was invited by the Lord Mayor Combe to preach the Spital Sermon.* He took me with him in the carriage. Never was church so crowded. Commoners, Peers, whigs, tories, filled every pew; I was favoured with a place in the Lord Mayor's. How few are now surviving of that multitude! Canning, Frere, Mackintosh, Bobus Smith, I recognized. Swarms of insignificant authors crowded the aisles and galleries; some of them doubtless wrote *articles by order*. When they went home, probably they were thinking what a good dinner Parr was enjoying with the Mayor. This thought took away part of their appetites, which returned the next day with the half-crown, and the pewter pot of porter mantling with emblematic froth. I did hope that the genial soul of Parr had by this time fairly escaped out of Purgatory, and that the pincers of his little persecutors had been laid by. Porson is not to be reprehended for smiling at him over his cups, but the Opium-eater is less easily to be pardoned his abusive intoxication. They who are incapable of doing

---

* Preached on Easter Tuesday, 1800.

justice may at least wish to do it, and may attempt it. No exercise is wholesomer.'

In some of the fragments we seem to have portions of a projected essay on poetic composition, and they might be pieced together without showing any more abrupt transitions than are met with in Landor's published writings. There is no warrant, however, for regarding them in this light, nor is it necessary to exhibit them except as unconnected passages. In the first Landor enlarges on the merits of Ovid, a favourite topic with him. Elsewhere he has made Petrarch say that of all the ancient Romans Ovid had the finest imagination; and in the 'Imaginary Conversations' there are endless allusions to his own liking for Ovid's poetry. The observations I shall now quote begin with a reference to people who find many faults in Ovid and discover none in Virgil.

IN PRAISE OF OVID.

' In the earlier [works] of Ovid there is greatly more poetical spirit than in the earlier of Virgil, and in my opinion all the *Eclogues* are not worth a single epistle of the Heroines. We must never suppose that the poet wrote the beginning in "Dido to Æneas":

   ' " Sic ubi fata vocant, udis abjectus in herbis
      Ad vada Mæandri concinnit albus olor."*

For such trash as this a schoolmaster would pull a boy's hair. In the turbulence of her grief unhappy Dido thought little about a white swan, living or dying, and knew not whether there were shallows on the Mæander, or even whether there were such a river in the world. How affecting is the real commencement of the epistle:

   ' " Non quia te nostra [sperem prece posse moveri,
      Alloquor]."

' Are there not here irrepressible sighs and irresistible sobs and hopeless anguish ? This poem had appeared before the Æneid, else we might believe that Ovid had copied in it the most beautiful part of that noble poem.

' There is more invention and imagination in Ovid than in any poet between Homer and Shakespeare. Witches and faeries and allegorical impersonations afford no proof of imagination or originality. We find them in succession. Their moulted feathers drop and repullulate periodically. A short allegory may be very charming ; a longer is insufferably

---

* Ovid, Heroid., vii. 1. See also Landor, Works, 1896, viii., p. 412.

tedious. Did anyone ever read the "Faery Queene" a single hour at a sitting, without stretching his legs out and his arms up, and the *ore rotundo* of a gape, silent or sonorous ?'

On the same sheet of paper are some remarks concerning the difference between fancy, imagination, and invention, not inaptly illustrated by references to English writers from Shakespeare to Southey. Wordsworth, in the preface to the volume of his poems published in 1815, had enlarged on the same topic. Landor writes :

' It appears to me that fancy is somewhat lighter than imagination. We often hear that he or she has fancies, never imaginations. Weak intellects are swayed by fancy ; stronger bring images before them. Nothing is more incorrect than the expression of Ben Jonson* in the verse :

' " Where sweetest Shakespeare, Fancy's child,
    Warbled his native woodnotes wild."

Shakespeare was no warbler, nor were wood-notes his, nor was there any wildness [in] even his earlier poems. On the contrary they were elaborate, and

---

* A *lapsus pennæ* ; the lines are Milton's. The same remark, with the name rightly given, is made by Landor elsewhere. See Works, 1876, v. 154.

the thoughts were often far-sought and quaint. He played with Fancy when he was adult, and only for the hour and in brief moments of it. Imagination, not Fancy, possessed him when he made Caliban his slave, and when he possest the heart of Miranda. His invention was more copious than in any other poet, as were his fancy and imagination more vivid. Both invention and imagination may exist in full vigour beyond the regions of poetry. Richardson, an author now neglected, created and imagined the characters of Clarissa and her persecutors, and placed them closely and distinctly before our eyes. He was a great inventor. Scott was more of a poet in his novels than in his poems, wherein he was also great. Southey was a true poet in his " Kehama " as in many of his other works. In his " Kehama " he has shown more imagination and invention than any other poet in the present or last century.'

In another fragment, without beginning or end, Landor has noted down some reflections on the nature of poetry, together with opinions on certain of his own contemporaries. The manuscript is in places illegible, but the *lacunæ* are of slight consequence. He says:

' For the larger works of poetry the requisites are conciseness without abruptness, comprehensiveness without diffuseness ; for the smaller a portion of these qualities under the presidence of grace. But above all things, affectation of novelty is to be avoided and never to be taken for originality. Nothing in poetry is original. The best poets have labored with the same conceptions. . . .* But it happens more frequently that the ideas spring up before him [the poet] without his consciousness. They have sprung up before others from generation to generation. Do you believe that the noble speech of Sarpedon to Glaucos† was never in the mind of others long before? The clashing of characters brought out those sparks in Shakespeare which will be unextinguished in the breast of millions to all eternity. Men before him have thought and felt somewhat of the same. There was earth before God moulded it into man.

'We must not overlook or undervalue our contemporaries, but it is safer to abstain from the praise of one or other, else we may be called negligent or indifferent or ignorant.

'We may walk back with impunity among the recently dead. We may revert to the "Ivan" and the "Casabianca" of Felicia Hemans; to Campbell's "Battle of Hohenlinden" and of "The Baltic"; we may accompany Southey, and acknowledge in his "Kehama" the most imaginative of our modern poets in whatever country they may have been

---

* A few words are illegible.

† Homer, 'Iliad,' xii.

flourishing.   In reading some of his earlier works you perhaps will say :

    ' " Lenibus atque utinam scriptis adjuncta foret
          vis !"

' Cowper was grave and intellectual, but never is prosaic as Wordsworth often is, for example in his dedication to Lord Lonsdale :

                ' " Illustrious peer
With high respect and gratitude sincere."

' Moore is caught gilding refined gold, yet in the midst of pleasantry there is tenderness and grace. . . .*   The " Lays of Rome " are vigorous ; his [Macaulay's] criticism and history are diluted epigrams, and are more ingenious than just.   I have not spoken of Scott, Wordsworth, and Byron. Scott superseded Wordsworth, and Byron superseded Scott, unjustly in both instances.   Scott had a wider range than either, and excelled in more qualities.'

---

      * A few words are illegible.

CHAPTER III.

LOVES AND FRIENDSHIPS.

'Certainly there is a middle state between love
and friendship, more delightful than either, but
more difficult to remain in.'

W. S. LANDOR.

'ROSE AYLMER'S hair.' This is the inscription
in Landor's unmistakable hand* on a small
paper packet containing a lock of hair of a
light amber tint, or, should one say, of sunlit
gold, and of a beautiful texture. Perhaps no
lines that Landor ever composed are better
known or more often quoted than the plaintive
elegy in which he mourned this young lady's
death :

> 'Ah! what avails the sceptred race,
> Ah! what the form divine.'

---

* The ink is of a peculiar kind which he sometimes used.

There is surely no need to repeat the rest; yet not everyone, it may be, who knows the lines by heart could rightly interpret the allusion to a 'sceptred' race. John Aylmer, Bishop of London in the latter half of the sixteenth century, is twice mentioned in Landor's 'Imaginary Conversations.' A note appended to that between Lord Brooke and Sir Philip Sidney reminds the reader that Bishop Aylmer was wont to play bowls after Sunday service, and that when censured by the over-devout for so doing, the good prelate replied: 'The Sabbath was made for man, and not man for the Sabbath.' Landor also liked the Bishop for his orthography, and cited his spelling of the words *monark* and *tetrark* as an example worthy to be imitated.

From Bishop Aylmer, as Landor believed, were descended the Irish peers who bear his name. The Honourable Rose Whitworth Aylmer was the only daughter of the fourth Baron Aylmer, and the sister of his successor, who was Governor-General of Canada from 1830 to 1835.

The story of Landor's acquaintance with Rose Aylmer has been touched on by Mr.

Forster, and with a finer sympathy by Mr. Colvin. There are one or two points, however, in regard to which a few words may be said. It was at Swansea, and, I think, in the autumn of 1796,* that Landor met Miss Aylmer. Her father had died in 1785, and she was living with Lady Aylmer at what was then a secluded watering-place, not yet bristling with the tall chimneys of copper smelting works. Landor was a young gentleman of one-and-twenty, Miss Aylmer being a few years younger. Born in October, 1779, she was now just seventeen.

I have been unable to find any portrait of Miss Aylmer. In Mr. Andrew Lang's collection of lyrics there is a picture of a ghost-like lady, which is supposed to represent 'that form divine'; but it is, I fear, merely a fancy sketch. A portrait of Lady Graves-Sawle, Miss Aylmer's niece, was published in the 'Book of Beauty' for 1840, and General Mackinnon, C.B., has an oil painting of her brother, General Lord Aylmer: no portrait of herself is discoverable. There is nothing but this lock of hair. Nor

* See Landor's poem, 'St. Clair,' in 'Dry Sticks,' p. 86.

have we any portrait of Landor at this period. He had already published two little volumes of poetry, had spent a year at Oxford and been rusticated, had obtained glimpses of fashionable life in London, and had now betaken himself to South Wales, to read Milton and Pindar. When not engaged in these studies or in field-sports, he cultivated a far from hopeless passion at Tenby, and at Swansea a sentimental friendship with Miss Aylmer. She was his companion in walks to Briton Ferry and along the banks of the River Tawey; and it was she who supplied a theme for the heroic narrative which made him known to some of the most distinguished writers of the day. For Miss Aylmer lent him 'The Progress of Romance,' by Clara Reeve, getting the book from the Swansea circulating library. In one of the stories told by that once fashionable authoress he found the framework of 'Gebir,' the work in which Southey discerned miraculous beauties and some of the most exquisite poetry in the English language; which, years afterwards, Shelley was never tired of reciting to whoever would listen; and which a Quarterly reviewer, in his blindness, pronounced to be 'a thing distressing to read and of an unconquerable obscurity.'*

Tenderly as Rose Aylmer's memory is evoked in the verses that Charles Lamb 'lived upon for weeks,' and fondly as Landor cherished the beautiful memento of those early days, there was more sentiment than passion in his devotion, and nothing of either, perhaps, in the girlish regard felt by Miss Aylmer for the young poet who was ready to worship at her shrine. Yet mourned she was and unforgotten all the days of his life; and even in old age he would transcribe and emend the poems he had written for her in his boyhood. One at least of them will be found among those now printed for the first time.

What is even more interesting than the verses is a letter of Landor's, which Lady Graves-Sawle allows me to quote here. It was written in reply to a question asked by her mother, Mrs. Paynter, and gives us, I think, for the first time an explicit allusion in Landor's own words to the 'torn romance' of his youth:

* *Quarterly Review*, 1837, p. 143.

'BATH,
'*Feb.*, 1853.

'DEAR MRS. PAYNTER,

'All this evening I have been trying to re-collect the verses, to which you alluded, to Rose Aylmer. I am quite certain I never wrote any of an amatory turn, nor ever offered a word of love to your lovely sister. After beating my brains, I picked up the only lines I wrote about her, until I heard, two years later, of her death. I took my boy's copy book (we had no Albums in those days) to show Mrs. Willoughby what I had written, the day before, on a forfeit I had won and had exacted on the evening of Twelfth Night. I will transcribe them for you ; my copy book was chiefly filled with Latin and Greek. I do not believe that any [? prize] was prefixt to the [verses]. Your sister had cut a nick at the end of her bonnet ribbon at Mrs. Thomas', where several girls and youths were. I picked up the little triangle, saying it was too precious to be lost, or for anyone to possess it without a contest, and proposed that we should draw lots for it. I gave the verses to Mrs. Thomas, and nobody else. I was not successful in the drawing. In the autumn of that year I left Swansea for Tenby.

'" Where all must love, but one can win the prize,
    The others walk away with tears and sighs.
    With tears and sighs let them walk off, while I
    Walk for three miles in better company."

' But I did not walk the three miles that morning,
or for many after. The more serious verses I wrote
six years later.

' " I draw with trembling hand my doubtful lot ;
   Yet where are Fortune's frowns, if *she* frown not
     From whom I hope, from whom I fear the
       kiss ?
   O gentle Love ! if there be ought beyond
   That makes the bosom calm, but leaves it fond,
     O let her give me that and take back this." '

       *   *   *   *   *

The reader may recollect, with some surprise,
that while the first of the two *poemetti* transcribed in this letter cannot be found anywhere
in Landor's published writings; the second was
printed among the verses to Ianthe. As will
presently be seen, there are other instances of
such unconscious or deliberate mystification.

Before the close of the last century Miss
Aylmer went out to India to stay with her
mother's sister, the wife of Sir Henry Russell,
a judge of the Supreme Court of Judicature in
Bengal.

   ' Where is she now ?   Called far away
    By one she dared not disobey,
    To those proud halls for youth unfit,
    Where princes stand and judges sit.'*

---

* Landor's ' Heroic Idyls,' p. 158.

Landor's verses seem to suggest that Miss Aylmer went to India rather against her will, but I know not if there is any warrant for this theory.   Sir Henry Russell was a noted man in his day.   Appointed by the Crown to a puisne judgeship in Bengal, he went out to India in the Company's ship *Earl Fitzwilliam*, reaching Calcutta in May, 1798, a few days after the new Governor-General, Lord Mornington, had taken over charge of his high office.   Lady Russell, with her niece Miss Aylmer and another niece, who afterwards married Sir Theophilus Metcalfe, followed Sir Henry some months later.

Of Miss Aylmer's uncle, the judge, one may read in old volumes of the *Asiatic Annual Register* how he would address the grand jury 'in an elegant, pertinent and perspicuous charge,' and how, on one occasion, he passed a capital sentence on a young Company's cadet who had set fire to a native's hut.   The judgment created no small sensation in Calcutta, and was referred to by a local poet:

> ' Truth and order seemed to shed a tear,
>   And Russell's voice still sounded in my ear.'*

---

* ' Calcutta: a Poem,' by J. J.   London, 1811.

But of Miss Aylmer's life after she said fare-well to Landor we know nothing. Doubtless she went to balls at Government House where she perhaps had a certain Colonel Arthur Wellesley as a partner. It is still more likely that she knew a lady whose charms have been celebrated by a great writer who, like Landor, was a Warwickshire man. Writing to Boswell in March, 1774, Dr. Johnson said: 'Chambers is either married, or almost married, to Miss Wilton, a girl of sixteen, exquisitely beautiful, whom he has with his lawyer's tongue persuaded to take her chance with him in the East.' Sir Robert Chambers resigned the Chief Justiceship of Bengal just before Sir Henry Russell took his seat on the bench; but he lived in India till his death in 1803.

The *Asiatic Register* for 1800 records the death, on March 3, of 'the Hon. Miss Aylmer, a young lady of great beauty and accomplish-ments.' She died of cholera:

> ' Where Ganges rolls his widest wave
> She dropped her blossom in the grave;
> Her noble name she never changed,
> Nor was her nobler heart estranged.'*

* Landor's verses in ' Heroic Idyls,' p. 158.

ROSE AYLMER'S TOMB AT CALCUTTA.

(From a Photograph.)

To face p. 72.

Her grave is in the cemetery in South Park
Street, Calcutta; and I am able to give a
sketch of the monument erected to her memory.
It bears the following inscription:

In MEMORY OF

THE HONOURABLE

ROSE WHITWORTH AYLMER,

WHO DEPARTED THIS LIFE

MARCH THE 2ND, A.D. 1800,

AGED 20 YEARS.

' What was her fate?   Long, long before her hour
Death called her tender soul by break of bliss,
From the first blossoms, from the bud of joy.
Those few our noxious fate unblasted leaves
In this unclement clime of human life.'

Possibly it was of Rose Aylmer's death that
Landor was thinking, when, years afterwards,
he wrote those mournful stanzas:

' My pictures blacken in their frames
As night comes on;
And youthful maids and wrinkled dames
Are now all one.

' Death of the day! a sterner Death
Did worse before;
The fairest form, the sweetest breath,
Away he bore.'

The lock of Rose Aylmer's hair, found in the cedar-wood desk nearly a hundred years after her death, was given to Landor by her half-sister, Mrs. Paynter. The gift was acknowledged in the lines:

'Beautiful spoils! borne off from vanquish'd death,
Upon my heart's high altar shall ye lie,
Moved but by only one adorer's breath,
Retaining youth, rewarding constancy.'*

Leigh Hunt has related how he and Landor made acquaintance—'as other acquaintances commence over a bottle'—when looking at a solitary hair stolen by some froward tourist from a lock of Lucretia Borghia's hair exhibited in the Ambrosian library at Milan.† There may be some whom the sight of this lock of Rose Aylmer's hair would lead to a more intimate knowledge of Landor. It would be a pathetic introduction.

Were it not for Landor's handwriting, one might have doubted to whom it belonged.

* 'Last Fruit off an old Tree,' p. 383.
† See Landor's verses, Works, 1876, viii. 92; and an article by Leigh Hunt, reprinted in his *London Journal*, April 22, 1835.

There are other 'beautiful spoils' that inspired his rhymes. Mention has already been made of tender passages at Tenby, where dwelt the Ione of his verse. Some of Ione's 'golden hairs, once mingled with my own,'* were also at one time among the trophies of his former loves. No trace of them, however, was found in his desk, nor was there anything that could surely be described as a memento of this 'gentle, young Ione,' whom he named with the nymphs in 'Gebir,' and later with the Nereids in 'Chrysaor':

'Sweet Ione, youngest born,
Of mortal race, but grown divine by song.'

On the other hand there is more than one visible reminiscence of another page of love in his life's history; the page, I think, which he recalled most often. I have already quoted the letter in which he referred to two miniatures to be kept for his sake, as he had kept them for theirs they represent. In another letter, written apparently a day or two later, that is, about the beginning of June, 1863, Landor said:

'The smaller miniature is a portrait of the Countess (*sic*) de Molandè, who came to visit me

* See Works, 1896, viii., pp. 77 and 296.

at my villa thirty years after. The smaller (*sic*) one is of her grand-daughter, since married to Mr. O'Donnell of Baltimore. The civil war in America makes me anxious about her, since no letter from her has reacht me lately.'

There were two miniatures in the desk, and any doubt arising from the confusion between smaller and larger is set at rest by the writing on the back of the larger one. Here is written in pencil, 'Miss de Sodre,' and in ink, the signature of the artist, 'C. Ford. Bath, 1849.' Miss de Sodre was the grand-daughter of the Countess de Molandè, who is pictured in the smaller and older miniature. This represents a charming girl, with laughter-loving eyes and pouting lips, cheeks radiant with health, and brown hair clustering in curls on her smooth brow :

> ' O thou whose happy pencil strays
>   Where I am call'd, nor dare to gaze,
>   But lower my eye and check my tongue ;
>   O, if thou valuest peaceful days,
>   Pursue the ringlet's sunny maze,
>   And dwell not on those lips too long.'

The lines are printed among the verses addressed to Ianthe in the volume published

Pauline

by Landor in 1831. They were most likely written some time before; though whether intended for a warning to the artist who painted this particular miniature is a problem that evades inquiry. What we do know is that the charming girl here depicted is the Ianthe of a cycle of love-lyrics which it is hard to match; Ianthe, whose pleasures sprang like daisies on the grass; 'she whom no Grace was tardy to adorn'; Ianthe of the cherisht form and heavenly smile; Ianthe of the white hand and warm, wet cheek; of happy days and fond regrets; Ianthe whose lovely name inspired the poet's song:

> 'And dwelling in the heart
> Forever falters at the tongue
> And trembles to depart.'

Ianthe's genealogy and descent may be traced in Burke's 'Landed Gentry.' Her maiden name was Sophia Jane Swift, and her great-great-grandfather was Godwin Swift, the uncle of the famous Dean. Landor, who once declared that he read 'The Tale of a Tub' oftener than any prose work in the English language, fell an easy victim to the fascinations of a gentler member of the family. Dean Swift, as we know from Alexander Pope,* had 'very particular eyes; they are quite azure as the heavens, and there is a very uncommon archness in them.' There may have been a family likeness.

Landor and his Ianthe met first, I think, at Clifton. Inside Landor's writing-desk is fastened an engraving after a sketch by S. Jackson of the view from Clifton Church, and he always associated that neighbourhood with memories of Ianthe:

'The mossy bank, dim glade and dizzy hight,
The sheep that, starting from the tufted thyme,
Untune the distant Church's mellow chime.'

Few poets who transmute their love affairs into song can be trusted to render a strictly impartial account either of raptures or torments. The loves of Landor and Ianthe, as related by Landor, may bear little resemblance, in some details of the story, to the truer record Ianthe could have given of their companionship. Still it is not difficult to make a fair guess at what happened. Of Landor, three years before his death, Browning wrote: 'Whatever he may profess, the thing he really loves is a pretty

* 'Spence's Anecdotes,' p. 135.

girl to talk nonsense with.' In such alluring pastime he had found solace and contentment, whatever else failed, all the days of his life; and who can doubt that he discoursed oceans of nonsense with the pretty Irish girl? How much of seriousness was mixed therein one cannot tell, but the fact is on record that Ianthe, whose wisdom and foresight can never be too highly commended, married not the heir of Ipsley Court in Warwickshire, but her cousin, Mr. Godwin Swifte, of Lionsden, County Kilkenny, and lived very happily with him. Even if she gave Landor more encouragement than should prudently have been accorded, who can blame the fair inciter of such exquisite lyrics? Even were Ianthe 'fond, but fickle and untrue,' literature is the richer by tender, sad complaints like these :

> ' Bid my bosom cease to grieve,
>   Bid these eyes fresh objects see,
> Where's the comfort to believe
>   None would once have rival'd me?
> What, my freedom to receive?
>   Broken hearts, are they the free?
> For another can I live
>   If I may not live for thee?'

That Ianthe was Miss Swift when Landor met her first is, I think, evident from more than one little poem, in which, as first printed, he calls her 'sweet maid.' Moreover, there are Latin verses, 'Ad Ianthen':

'O per virgineos, carissima dona, capillos,
    O mihi virgineâ non data dona manu.'

According to family tradition, Ianthe's marriage took place in 1803. Among the hitherto unpublished poems printed in another part of the present volume there is one which seems to describe a highly indiscreet endeavour to see and converse with the lady after her hand had been finally bestowed on a happier rival. Perhaps it was no more than a dream.

When seeking for autobiography in Landor's writings there are frequent pitfalls to beware of. Landor once accused himself—and not altogether unjustly—of being a horrible confounder of historic facts. There was usually, he confessed, one history that he had read and another that he had invented. Invention sometimes played its part in his verses, as it does in those of other poets who might be named. And there was another source of mystification.

In one of his dialogues Landor unconsciously borrowed a notion from Sir Thomas Browne's 'Religio Medici.' 'A misery there is in affection that whom we truly love like our own selves, we forget their looks, nor can our memory retain the Idea of their faces.' So Sir Thomas Browne wrote; and Landor makes Filippo Lippi repeat, as a saying of the corsair from Tunis who carried him into captivity, 'Alas! when we most love the absent, when we most desire to see her, we try in vain to bring her image back to us.' Landor, I suspect, could not always bring to mind, when nearly a long lifetime afterwards he revised a poem for the printer, the name of her to whom it had been addressed. Then, again, he would alter a set of verses, intended originally for one fair enchantress, so as to make them apply to another. To me it seems indisputable that a few, at any rate, of the poems labelled 'To Ianthe' in the volume printed in 1831 were actually inspired, in the previous century, by Ione. One in particular, when published in 1804—it was doubtless written some years earlier—contained verses which were omitted in 1831, and which, though they may have referred to Ione,

would be altogether inadmissible in a poem
about Ianthe.   This is a point which Landor's
future editors must not overlook.   As an instance
of the permutation of names in Landor's love
poetry the lines

> ' Thank Heaven, Neæra, once again
>   Our lips in ardent kisses meet,'

may be quoted.   That is how they were printed
in 1802, and again in ' Heroic Idyls,' 1863; but
in Mr. Forster's two editions (1846 and 1876)
Neæra becomes Ianthe.   In the same way
Psyche alternates with *Zoe* in the verses
beginning

> ' Against the rocking mast I stand.'

Last of all there are not wanting grounds for
the suspicion that someone who harboured a
grudge against the charming Ianthe was re-
sponsible for a use of her name in a way wholly
unwarranted by the facts.   ' I printed,' Landor
wrote to Southey, ' whatever was marked with
a pencil by a woman who loved me, and I consulted all her caprices.'   Some commentators
have supposed that Ianthe herself was the
' woman who loved me,' and who made the
selection.   On the other hand, in another letter

to the same address, Landor said: 'But, Southey, I love a woman who will never love me, and am beloved by one who never ought.' Here be mysteries not to be fathomed.

So I do not attach very great significance to a list, in Landor's hand, of 'verses to Ianthe.' When he sent a copy of his poems to Miss Mary Boyle, he protested that *all* the amatory ones were ideal. 'Someone,' he said, 'has fancied that Ianthe (stolen by Byron) is only Jane with the Greek Θ. What noodles are commentators!' Still, the manuscript list may suffice to clear up some perplexities. It shows, for instance, that the beautiful lines to J. S., at whose identity Mr. Colvin would not even hazard a guess, were meant for Ianthe, being addressed to Jane Sophia when she was Madame de Molandè. They lend such charming colour to the portrait of Ianthe that I cannot refrain from transcribing them :

> ' Many may yet recall the hours
> That saw thy lover's chosen flowers
> Nodding and dancing in the shade
> Thy dark and wavy tresses made ;
> On many a brain is pictured yet
> Thy languid eye's dim violet ;

> But who among them all foresaw
> How the sad snows that never thaw
> Upon that head one day should lie,
> And love but glimmer from that eye?'

And one would not willingly lose the romance that might be woven from the chain of verses to an idealized Ianthe. Remember only that Ianthe does not invariably stand for Miss Swift, afterwards Mrs. Swifte (her cousin and husband added an *e* to the name), and as pretty a tale of love may be told as ever poet feigned. The Ianthe of our imagination had a pleasing, yet perhaps not a very safe method, or to be commended to a susceptible generation, of compelling her poet's attention:

> ' Ianthe took me by both ears, and said:
> " You are so rash, I own I am afraid.
> Prop, or keep hidden in your heart, my name,
> But be your love as lasting as your fame." '

Nor is it only once that the lover—the imaginary lover—finds himself in such tolerable durance. He repeats some of his Latin verses, whereupon ' she held me by both ears till I gave her the English.' In the language of Tibullus and Ovid the lines run:

'Vita brevi est fugitura, prior fugitura voluptas,
  Hoc saltem exiguo tempore duret amor.'

And, Englished by the audacious versifier, they become:

'Too soon, Ianthe, life is o'er,
  And sooner beauty's playful smile.
Kiss me, and grant what I implore,
  Let love remain that little while.'

One of Landor's 'Hellenics' ends with a dubitation concerning a kiss:

'A swain averr'd
That he descried in the deep wood a cheek
At first aslant, then lower, then eclipst.
Another said it was not in the wood,
But in the grotto near the water-fall,
And he alone had seen it.
          The dispute
Ran high; a third declared that both were
  wrong.'

One is so apt to be mistaken at such times, and the better way is not to look.

To return to the veritable Ianthe. Much may be gathered about her life and character from a little volume of reminiscences written by her son. Her first husband, the father of her five children, died in 1814. She mourned him sincerely, and her acute grief brought on an attack of brain fever. Then followed a year or two of consolable widowhood, during which time Mrs. Swifte, young, pretty, and with a good income at her disposal, helped to embellish the reception-rooms of various provincial towns and watering-places. Her son relates that on one occasion his mother's power of fascination was exerted in the interests of what local opinion looked upon as justice. Local opinion ran high in favour of two prisoners about to be tried on some capital charge. Ianthe resolved that they should escape the law's extreme penalty; and to that end invited the learned judge—no other than Lord Norbury—and the grand jury to dinner, after which there was dancing. The judge vowed he would dance with the lovely widow as long as he had a leg to stand on; and his Lordship, we are to infer, was so mollified by the gracious attention he received, that, when the trial came on, he gave the prisoners the benefit of a doubt. Long before this, of course, Landor had married Miss Julia Thuillier; and the same year that made Ianthe a widow saw him, his mundane estate sadly encumbered by rash experiments at Llanthony, and by experiments still more unwise in litigation, an exile from his country, and estranged for weeks together from his young wife. That passing discord was quickly composed, and for the space of twenty years husband and wife lived together in Italy, except for a few months in 1832, when Landor revisited England.

Toward the end of 1829 he again met Ianthe, now for the second time a widow. In 1816 she had married the Count Lepelletier de Molandè, a Norman nobleman, who in his youth had been page to the beautiful and unfortunate Princesse de Lamballe, and who afterwards, emigrating to England, was attached to the person of George IV. He died in or about 1827; and Madame de Molandè, going to Florence in 1829, renewed her acquaintance with Landor. Writing to his sister Ellen, he styled this lady the dearest of all the friends he ever had or ever should have. Neither time nor bereavement had impaired her beauty, and she was now being entreated by two ardent suitors—an English earl and a French duke, to venture on a third essay in matrimony.

'I wonder not,' Landor wrote, ' that youth remains with you :'

> ' Where could he find such fair domains,
>   Where bask beneath such sunny eyes ?'

He also addressed some verses to ' Madame de Molandè about to marry the Duke of Luxemburg '; but neither this nor the other match came off. During her residence in Florence, the Countess visited the Landors at their Fiesolan Villa. Moreover, at her host's request, she planted four mimosa - trees in his garden, round the spot marked out by him as his last resting-place. Nor did Landor shrink from composing a suitable epitaph :

> ' Lo ! where the four mimosas blend their shade
>   In calm repose at last is Landor laid ;
>   For ere he slept he saw them planted here
>   By her his soul had ever held most dear.'

In 1832, when Landor revisited England after an absence of eighteen years, he found Madame de Molandè living at Brighton, ' in the midst,' he wrote, ' of music, dancing, and fashionable people turned Radicals,' and he stayed a couple of days at her house. Of further meetings there is no record till Landor had left his wife and children in a fit of inextinguishable anger, and had once more taken up his abode among the 'peopled hills' of Bath. There also Madame de Molandè settled down for a while, and often helped him to bear the burden of advancing age. At Bath Mr. Forster was presented to the Countess. 'Even when I first saw her,' he wrote, 'a bright, good-humoured Irish face was all her beauty, but youth still lingered in her eyes and hair.' All too soon was Landor deprived of this and many another consolation in his solitude. The Laureate Southey, the accomplished Francis Hare, the generous Joseph Ablett, the glorious Lady Blessington—all were gone; and in a letter, dated August 3, 1851, Landor wrote:

'I have lost my beloved friend of half a century, Jane, the Countess de Molandè. She died at Versailles on the last of July after sixteen hours' illness. This most affecting intelligence was sent me by her son William, who was with her at her last hour. She will be brought over to the family vault, in County Meath, of her first husband, Swifte, great-great-grandson of the uncle of the Dean of St. Patrick's. I hoped she might have seen my grave. Hers I shall never see, but my thoughts will visit it often. Though other friends have died in other days (why cannot I help this running into verse?) one grave there is whose memory sinks and stays.'

In the volume of 'Heroic Idyls' is an elegy, beginning:

'I dare not trust my pen, it trembles so.'

The manuscript of these lines is now in the British Museum.

With many among Landor's friends, the love he bore them descended from generation to generation. Of Ianthe's daughters by her first husband, the elder, Jane Christiana, was married in 1835 to the Chevalier Sergio de Macèdo, the Brazilian Minister in London. The younger, Maria, had married, five years earlier, the Chevalier Louis de Pereira Sodre, the Brazilian Minister at the Vatican. Madame de Pereira Sodre died in 1836, leaving a daughter, Luisina, whose girlhood was passed under the care of the Countess de Molandè. Miss de Pereira Sodre became a great favourite of Landor's at Bath, and, as already stated, her portrait was found in his writing-desk. Several little poems were addressed to this young lady. In one of them, published in the *Keepsake* for

1853, and also in 'Last Fruit,' mention is made of her having waltzed with the Emperor of Austria at Vienna, to whose court her uncle was at one time accredited:

'Blush not to have been so chosen: 'twas that blush
Which won the choice: 'twas not Pereira's name,
'Twas not De Sodre's, not Macèdo's.'

There are verses also on Luisina's portrait:

' Afar was I when thou wast born
More than one country to adorn,
My Luisina! and afar
From me now shines thy morning star.'

A poetical exhortation was likewise addressed to the young lady when she was about to visit Paris, bidding her ' Listen not to the Frenchman's tongue.'

A further reminiscence of Luisina, coupled with one of another friend, is preserved in a letter of Landor's to Mr. Forster. He was enlarging on the intelligence and amiability of his dog Pomero, and proceeds:

' Last evening I took him to hear Luisina de Sodre play and sing. She is my friend, the Countess de Molandè's grand-daughter. . . . Pomero was deeply affected and lay, close to the pedal, on her gown, singing in a great variety of tones, not always in time. It is unfortunate that he always *will* take a part where there is music, for he sings even worse than I do.'

Among the memorials found in Landor's desk was a tuft of poor Pomero's hair ; Pomero, who for thirteen years was his master's inseparable companion, and whose virtues were celebrated both in English and Latin. Here is his epitaph :

'CANEM AMICUM SUUM EGREGIE CORDATUM
QUI APPELLATUS FUIT POMERO,
SAVAGIUS LANDOR INFRA SEPELIVIT.'

'Pray for me and Pomero,' Landor wrote to Miss Boyle ; 'some people are wicked enough to believe that we shall never meet again.' Pomero had been sent to Bath from Italy. There was not an older family, his master vowed, in all Bologna. 'His ancestors preceded the Bentivoglios, and were always staunch republicans.'

CHAPTER IV.

SOME OLD LETTERS.

'How carelessly people say "I am delighted to hear from you." No other language has this beautiful expression.'

W. S. Landor.

By the kindness of a lady to whom Walter Savage Landor was greatly attached, I am able to print a number of letters of an earlier date than those addressed to Dr. Walker. A little while before he left his citron groves of Fiesole and the beloved villa, where

'By the lake Boccaccio's "Fair Brigade"
Beguiled the hours and tale for tale repaid,'

he enjoyed the pleasure of meeting Miss Rose Aylmer's half-sister, Mrs. Paynter, who, with her daughter, a second 'Rose from that same stem,' came to stay for a time in Florence.

Out of fond recollections of the past, as well as from the enjoyment of present felicities such as he ever found in gracious company, there quickly arose an affectionate esteem that comforted his loneliness for another quarter of a century. And for Miss Rose Paynter, a little girl when he first knew her, but just released from the nursery, the gallant, kindly gentleman, now hard on sixty, entertained feelings not unlike the loving regard of Epicurus, in the 'Imaginary Conversations,' for his charming pupils in philosophy, Leontion and Ternissa. Need it be said that for her also there was poetry in profusion? In 1840 Miss Paynter's portrait, engraved from a painting in oils by Fisher, appeared in the 'Book of Beauty,' along with verses by Landor. Six years later, on her marriage to Sir Charles Graves-Sawle,

> 'She upon her wedding day
> Carried home my tenderest lay.'

Later still, more verses had to be written in honour of a third Rose.

The letters will speak for themselves. The first is addressed to Mrs. Paynter, the others to Miss Rose Paynter, now Lady Graves-Sawle.

To Mrs. Paynter at Rome.

'FLORENCE,
'*April* 3 [? 1833].

'DEAR MRS. PAYNTER,

'. . . Nothing would have been more un-conscionable in me than to have expressed a wish to hear from you while at Rome for the first time; and nothing can be kinder than for you to cast a thought on me from amidst so many wonders and reflections. . . . Miss Mackenzie* is so charmed with you and the twin roses, for I will not allow one to be more rosy than the other. They will care no more for having charmed her than for having charmed me, who am rather the older of the two old women, though there cannot be more than twenty or thirty years' difference, which is no great matter in such antiquities as you are getting used to. Since you left Florence I have rarely gone within the gates. Yesterday I finished the planting of two thousand vines, and in the autumn I shall plant as many more, besides seventy olives. I did think of going to England, but if I do, I shall return by November. Francis Hare is certainly the best informed as well as the best natured man you will meet in Italy. He will probably leave Rome about the same time as you do, but you take contrary directions. I am losing all my friends.

---

* Miss Mackenzie of Seaforth.

Mr. Brown,* an intelligent and most friendly man, is gone to England with a resolution never to return to Italy.   Mr. James† goes to-morrow with the same resolution.   I cannot bear the idea of seeing anything for the last time.   There is something in those two monosyllables that weighs very heavily on the heart ; more heavily than volumes of school divinity.   *Coragio, coragio.*   We must not talk in this manner.   Have we not both of us outlived the Last Days of Pompeii ?

'When you are at Naples, you will hear something of old Mathias, the man who wrote a sort of satire called " The Pursuit of Literature."   He now writes sonnets ; Italian ones, too.   When I was at Naples he inspired me, as you shall see.

> ' The piper's music fills the street,
> The piper's music makes the heat
> Hotter by ten degrees ;
> Hand us a sonnet, dear Mathias,
> Hand us a sonnet, cool and dry as
> Your very best, and we shall freeze.'

*   *   *   *   *

To Miss Rose Paynter.

' BATH,

' *December*, 1838.

DEAR ROSE,

'It is only the pleasure you are enjoying at Paris that would at all reconcile your circle here to

---

* Mr. Charles Armitage Brown, the friend of Keats.
† Mr. G. P. R. James, the novelist.

the loss of you, the bitterness of which at the first moments overflowed a little way beyond them. There were too many thoughts and too perplexing ones at bidding you farewell—I do not remember whether there was a voice to utter them: if there was it was forced into the service by a hard impressment.

' Kenyon tells me that Southey is going to take a second wife, Miss Caroline Bowles.*   She is represented as extremely amiable—not very young, nor should she be.   Southey is himself in his sixty-fifth year.   Surely he might see the mellow fruit on the *espalier* without any hasty eagerness to gather it. Surely, having been married once, and happily—— But in fear of running too far into the romantic, I will only say, I think I should have liked him rather the better had he been contented to stop short of matrimony.   However, he is a more judicious and a better man than I am, and I trust his choice will be conducive to his happiness.   In human life there is but one important event—may God prosper it to all my friends.

' You tell me there are no pretty women in Paris. Pretty women, I fancy, are reserved to be the ornaments of celebrated reigns.   In the commencement of Napoleon's career I remember Madame Tallien, Madame Recamier and Pauline.   The Duchesse de Grammont was handsome, rather past her perfection, but retaining a part of her bloom and all her graces.

---

* The marriage took place on June 5, 1839.

If you meet her you will be pleased with her. I cannot promise you quite so much in Lady Harriet d'Orsay, if you converse with her more than once.

' When Southey was appointed Poet-Laureate, it was understood that he should not be obliged to write any birthday verses, as had always been done before. When you appointed me to the same office the law was not very clearly laid down—I may shuffle, and am half inclined. However, you shall have as little as ever was offered on a similar occasion. I believe the 19th was the martyrdom of St. Agnes—never mind if I am wrong. The poets have as great a power as tyrants have, and can order an execution or a reprieve *ad libitum*.

> ' Slain was Agnes on the day
>   That we bless for Rose's birth ;
> Heaven, who took a Saint away,
>   Sent an Angel down to Earth.

' I have been spending a few days with my friend Hare in Berkshire. The house* was built by Inigo Jones—well adapted for Italy, better for Africa. The cold was intense, and I slept in a bed large enough for a company of comedians. Dear Rose,
' Your sincere, affectionate friend,
' W. S. L.'

---

* Westwood Way House, where Francis Hare was then living. In another letter Landor said the house would have done passably well for Naples, and better for Timbuctoo.

To Miss Rose Paynter.

'[BATH,]
'*March*, 1839.

'DEAR ROSE,

'At last I am able to send you a little book*
to occupy you on your voyage homeward. Do not
censure me for representing Giovanna of Naples
as an amiable and virtuous woman — her true
character. In regard to the murder of her husband there is no more doubt of her innocence than
there is of Mary Stuart's guilt. Giannone,† the
most dispassionate and impartial of historians, and
no favourer of Popes and Princes, mentions with
admiration her prudence, her genius, and her
gentleness of disposition, and repudiates the accusations brought against her by the blind vehemence
of an adverse faction. Boccaccio and Petrarcha in
their private letters are profuse in their praises of
her, and bitterly lament over her unmerited mis-
fortunes. They had been at her court before and
after her marriage. Now Petrarcha was somewhat

---

* 'Andrea of Hungary and Giovanna of Naples,'
by W. S. Landor. London, R. Bentley, 1839.

† Pietro Giannone's 'Civil History of Naples'
was translated into English, early in the last
century, by Captain Ogilvie. Landor also quotes
this writer's defence of Giovanna of Naples in his
'Essay on Petrarcha.' Works, 1876, viii. 442.

addicted to censoriousness, and to conceal the failings of ladies was not among the habitudes of Boccaccio.   You will be inclined to pray that I may not have another sprained ankle,* if a couple of Dramas are to spring out of bran and vinegar, and you must read them.

'I have been reading the "Old Men's Tales." Admirable! admirable!

'Amidst the amusements of Paris you can have little time for study, and much that you would read would shock you as unprincipled. The harp of De Beranger, the only poet, is strung only for Paris. Lamartine is a mere versifier, fantastically grave, and epigrammatically devout. Mignet, De Tocqueville and Cousin write for politicians. Do you ever meet with any of these authors? If they wish to keep up the illusion, they should rarely come into sight. We soon discover, when we step up close to it, of how petty materials the most solid granite is composed. Among their smaller authors it would be well if they exposed only the sugar and water that catch flies, without the poison that intoxicates and kills them. Exaggeration has

---

* 'He who sprains an ankle breaks a resolution. I sprained my ankle a week ago. . . . On Sunday after tea I began a drama on Giovanna di Napoli (God defend us from the horrid sound, Joan of Naples!).' Landor to Mr. Forster, October, 1838.

always been attractive. Voltaire alone is exempt from this fault. No language is purer or more perfect. We have no Bossuet, no Massillon. Milton, our only great proseman, is not always great as they are, although some pages of his are worth nearly all they ever wrote. In his " Treatise on Prelacy " are these words—printed, of course, as prose—" When God commands to take the trumpet and blow a dolorous or thrilling blast, it rests not in man's will what he shall say, or what he shall conceal."*   Is there anything more solemn or august in the whole range of poetry ?

' When years have stored your mind with obser-vation, you will continue to prefer Goldsmith to Bulwer, Miss Edgeworth to Lady Morgan, Madame de Sevigné to Chateaubriand : in other words, the very best to the very worst. Well and wisely has Boileau said : " *Rien n'est beau que le vrai, le vrai seul est aimable.*"

' I am going into Devonshire. Should I happen to see a small cottage and garden to let, I hope to gather my own gooseberries and radishes, and plant my own rose-tree. O, that I could once more enjoy the noble terraces of Sorrento, or my own at Fiesole, no less delightful. Sorrento, I may perhaps ; the other, never. I must break my promise with my

---

* Landor had a great liking for this quotation, and more than once printed it in the form of blank verse. See Works, 1876, v. 561 ; viii. 389.

four beautiful mimosas, to sit among them as long as I live on condition that they continue to scatter their sweet blossoms over me afterwards. These now only fall on the myrtles and oleanders, "plants of my hand and children of my care." Some of the oleanders were seven feet high when I left Tuscany, starring the ground and refreshing the air with their flowers.

'I once occupied the small apartment of Marie Antoinette at the Petit Trianon for a fortnight.* The windows were of a single pane, and overlooked the English or rather Chinese garden. Happy days! but not for memory. I have been writing for some hours; none of your many friends think of you oftener or more affectionately than that tiresome old scribbler,

'W. S. LANDOR.'

To Miss Rose Paynter.

'[BATH,]
'*May*, 1839.

'DEAR ROSE,
　　'So you have met Lord Brougham. He has not quite so amiable or tranquil a face as Lamartine. In plain truth it is quite the worst, and very nearly the ugliest physiognomy in existence. It has, however, one advantage over its proprietor—it does not lie.

---

* This was in 1802. See Forster's 'Life,' i. 174.

'When you visit Chantilly next, remember me affectionately to my old friends, the carp. When I saw them above thirty years ago, they were grayer than I was. Assure them that if I now wear their colours, it is not out of compliment to them. Nevertheless I follow them closely in their main opinion, which is always to keep out of hot water. . . .'

To Miss Rose Paynter.

'GORE HOUSE,
'*June*, 1839.

'. . . . An odd thing happened to me which I must tell you. I had given the *Examiner**** some remarks on Lord Brougham in which I brought down Bonaparte from the stilts on which our traitors have placed him. Prince Louis Napoleon, Montauban, and Persigny had been conversing with me in admirable good humour, when something was said by Lady Blessington about an article in I know not what paper. "*Apropos*," said Louis, "I owe many thanks to the author of the *Examiner* for his notice of the Emperor." Luckily he had forgotten that my name was at the bottom. I could not help smiling. They say he is no fool——he looks like one, which is unusual in that family. . . .'

---

* The article in the *Examiner* is reprinted in Landor's Works, 1876, v. 553.

To Miss Rose Paynter.

> ' [LONDON,]
> ' *June*, 1840.

' . . . . I sat at dinner [at Gore House] by Charles Forester, Lady Chesterfield's brother. In the last hunting season Lord Chesterfield, wanting to address a letter to him, and not knowing exactly where to find him, gave it to D'Orsay to direct it. He directed it—Charles Forester, one field before the hounds, Melton Mowbray. Lord Alvanley took it, and (he himself told me) gave it to him on the very spot.

Miss Caldwell* is returned from the sea-side—*fanciullesca fresca, fresca.* " Sure, Landor, it is a beautiful book, your ' Periwinkle and Asparagus ' ; but faith ! I've no time to read it." Yesterday Colonel Napier,† who is not imaginative, told me this. " Sure, we have been to see St. John's latter end—mighty odd name, is it not ?—there beyond the Pope's." " The Vatican ?" " Not an idea of

---

* ' My earliest Bath friend, Miss Caldwell, sister to dear, good Lady Belmore, of whose death I so lately wrote to you, died a few days ago. I had known them since the beginning of the century.' Landor to Mr. Forster, February 6, 1854.

† Sir William Napier, the historian of the Peninsular War.

it." "Perhaps you mean the Quirinal?" "The Quillinan, sure I know the name as well as our own house. James, put the Campanile on the table."

'Bess Caldwell was a well-known and loved Mrs. Malaprop. She lived with her sister, the Dowager Countess of Belmore, at Bath. Sir William Gell, when they were at Naples, compiled—and I believe published—a book called "Caldwelliana" of her remarkable sayings. Hayward's very clever essay mentions her as having said, "She had been to see the house where Ariosto lived with the widow of Charles the First."* She was a very intimate friend of my mother's.'

In the spring of 1841 Landor went to Paris to meet his second son. 'Imagine my surprise,' he wrote to Mr. Forster (May 6, 1841), 'that any among the literary men knew even of my existence. Nothing can exceed the attention I receive from them. If their civilities are sufficient to make a place agreeable, I ought to be quite contented at Paris.' The amenities of the trip are described in the following letter.

---

* She was thinking of Alfieri and the Countess of Albany. See *Edinburgh Review*, July, 1861.

To Miss Rose Paynter.

'PARIS,

' [*May*, 1841].

'. . . I was invited to a sitting of the Institute, Cousin in the chair. Mignet, the great historian of the Revolution, and perpetual President, made an admirable speech on Merlin de Douai. Thiers was present. His countenance is like a mangy rat's. M. Colmarke, private secretary to Talleyrand, introduced me to Ledru, the Erskine of France. He conducted Lady Bulwer's case, and has undertaken the defence of the wretched fools who conspired against Louis Philippe. I called on him yesterday, and he came out to see me and took me into his library, and after many civilities asked me if I would like to see the most noted man of France, meaning Vidocq. I said yes. He was admitted. He appears to be about sixty years old; wonderfully strong and of a physiognomy mild and intelligent. Ledru told me he was very trustworthy. On a former occasion Ledru had undertaken his defence, on condition that he gave 1,000 francs to the poor ; he performed his engagement honorably.

' I have never anywhere received so much kindness and civility. I have been introduced to many literary ladies, but I neither know their works nor remember their names. On Monday the Princess Czartoryski has promised I shall meet Madame Recamier and la Guiccioli. . . .'

To Miss Rose Paynter.

'*July* 16, 1842.

'. . . To-morrow I go with Lord Pembroke to Brighton, where I leave him. As soon as I have sealed this I will pay my respects to your uncle and aunt, Lord and Lady Aylmer. Afterwards I make a visit by appointment to a most extraordinary personage, the Countess Vespucci, the only lineal descendant of the discoverer of America—of North America, at least. She began her career by escaping from a convent at sixteen, and by placing herself at the head of the insurgents. She received, in the first engagement, a severe sabre cut on her head, a ball broke her arm, and she was left on the field of battle. She continues singularly beautiful, and she has the longest and finest hair I ever saw. Her genius is quite as extraordinary as her beauty and courage. She has had many offers of marriage, but appears more disposed to deprive others of their liberty than to surrender her own.

'The Duc de Guiche is the handsomest man I ever saw. What poor animals other men seem in the presence of him and D'Orsay. He is also full of fun, of anecdote, of spirit and of information. The sorrowful death of the Duke of Orleans* was

---

* Ferdinand, Duc d'Orleans, eldest son of King Louis Philippe, died on July 13, 1842, from injuries sustained in a fall from his cabriolet, while driving in the Champs Elysées.

rather a source of satisfaction to him. This vexed me, not only because the Duke of Orleans was a brave and kind-hearted young man, but because his death must be the bitterest grief to a most affectionate and virtuous mother. But politics make all men selfish, cold and calculating. To-day it will be amusing to meet the heads of both parties at dinner: the Duc de Guiche, the Tankervilles, Lord Lyndhurst, Lord Abinger, Lord Brougham, etc., etc. Some of these people are desperately stupid, some villainously dishonest; nevertheless they do not take away my appetite nor injure my digestion. Quiet Bath suits me better. I met Maclise at dinner at Dickens's. Landseer was at Gore House on Wednesday.

' Yours affectionately,
' W. S. L.'

To Miss Rose Paynter.

' WARWICK,
' *Sunday Night* [*July*, 1843].

' DEAR ROSE,

'. . . . Now for the first time my poetry deserves the greater part of a smile from you. At Mrs. Crampton's on Thursday our friend* (rather fond of causing occasionally a slight trepidation)

---

* The late Mr. James Edward Fitzgerald, C.M.G., Accountant-General, New Zealand.

desired, in a laughing way, that I would write his epitaph in case he happened to be lost in the British Channel as he boated to Devonshire. I wrote on the spot four Greek verses, of which there are versions on the other side of the paper. . . .

> ' Beloved by all Fitzgerald lies
> Where the sea waves for ever moan ;
> The dear delight of maiden eyes
> Is now embraced by Nymphs alone.'

To Miss Rose Paynter.

' [BATH,]
' *September* 3, 1845.

' DEAR R.,

'You have taken the right view of F——. What I had written on his poem was little different to that which I wrote to himself. I had remarked the absolute want of variety and invention in Byron, his model. Without these no poet can rise above a secondary station. Shakespeare took many of his characters and stories from other writers ; nevertheless his originality is greater and more exuberant than any other poet's. He breathed life into what he had formed out of the earth, and gave his fresh creation the universe for inheritance. The great poet must be conversant with a great variety of sentient beings and in a great variety of feelings, thoughts, and situations. He must keep them totally distinct from himself, and project them far before him. *Striking* characters, as they are called, are easily portrayed. A boy can draw a giant or a mountain, but how much care and ability is required, even in the greatest master, to catch the sparkles of a fountain or to calm the breast with a still and overshadowed water. The greatest achievements of poetry make no impression on ordinary minds. Tens of thousands were animated by the battles of the " Iliad " for one who struck his brow at the agony of Priam, or who prayed for the return of Hector when he lifted up his child, frightened at the radiance of his helmet. The last words of Lear that rive a great heart may perhaps be the ridicule of a less. Othello has been hated and execrated by more than have admired or pitied him. I once heard a man call him a coward, and it drove me into a gross imprudence, not to say indecorum.

' You might as well have thrown Kenyon's letter into the fire with mine. I had forgotten all its contents but his breach of promise, for which I intend to prosecute him.

' Tell Fred never to use the American word *realize* for *comprehend* or *conceive.*

' If there is a lodging cheap or dear to be procured at Budleigh I will take it from the eighth of September, the day of the Blessed Virgin, as I find it in the almanack, until Monday, the twenty-second, which I find in the same authority is the flight of Mahomet. My lodging must be open to

the sea, and have good water, my only beverage.
I intend to be at church on Sunday, and may reach
Budleigh that evening.

' Affectionately yours,
'W. S. L.'

To Mrs. Sawle.

'[1847.]

' MY DEAR, KIND, HOSPITABLE FRIEND,

'I reached Exeter after one, and had no
other accident but leaving my guide-book and gold
spectacles. I must disburse half my patrimony for
another pair. Vexatious! as I have six or seven
pairs already.

'It is useful and providential to have met with
some accident which turned my mind for an instant
from my regrets at leaving Ristormel.* Dear
Ristormel! its hanging woods, its sheltered gardens,
its warm summer-house. In all these, my past
days come back to me. I wish I could lift up face
to face the little Rosebud this morning. I can
fancy her splendid new sash falling over my elbow,

---

* Ristormel in Cornwall, where Mr. and Mrs.
Sawle (now Sir Charles and Lady Graves-Sawle)
were living.

'Known as thou art to ancient fame,
   My praise, Ristormel, shall be scant ;
The Muses gave thy sounding name,
   The Graces thy inhabitant.'

' Last Fruit off an old Tree.'

and her soft, cool little hand forbidding the approaches of my lips. God's blessings on her. . . .

'I have sent Mrs. Paynter the ' Reminiscences of Talleyrand." No memoirs (and memoirs are the *forte* of French literature) are comparable to this work. They were collected by Mons. Colmarke, the Prince's secretary. He is dead, and they are edited by his widow. I was very intimate with them both when I was in Paris, and she has made me a present of Talleyrand's spectacles. People like to keep themselves warm with the hatreds that cling about them. I confess I feel a relief in being able to think better than I used to think of this extraordinary man. I thought him much wiser but not much better than the statesmen of our own country and of the Continent who were contemporaries.

'My vision rests upon Ristormel. There is nothing half so pleasant to dwell upon.

'Believe me,

'Your affectionate old friend,

'W. S. L.'

To Mrs. Sawle.

'[BATH,]

'*September* 12, 1849.

'. . . My brother Charles died tranquilly. He was at once the strongest, the handsomest and the wittiest man I ever knew. His family are well provided for ; at seventy our portmanteaux are locked, and our carpet-bags can hold little more. I am quite ready to start whenever I am called.*

'I may never see dear Ristormel again unless in dreams; but I trust early in October to see what gave Ristormel all its charms.

'The Grammonts and D'Orsay are desirous that I should write *in latin* an epitaph on my kind old friend Lady Blessington. I detest latin epitaphs, but obey. Death commits a sacrilege when he breaks into a friendship of twenty - two years' standing. She is buried in a wood of old chesnuts at St. Germain. There was enough money from her sale to pay all her debts, and to leave £3,000 to her nieces. They will continue to live with the Duchesse de Grammont. . . .'

The Countess of Blessington died on June 4, 1849. Landor was one of her oldest friends:

' Thou sleepest, not forgotten nor unmourn'd
Beneath the chesnut shade of Saint Germain;
Meanwhile I wait the hour of my repose.'

So he wrote in a little elegy, printed first in the *Examiner*. The Latin epitaph may be found in 'Last Fruit,' with an English translation. It ended:

' Venit Lutetiam Parisiorum Aprili mense:
Quarto Junii die supremum suum obiit.'

---

* The Rev. Charles Landor died in July, 1849.

In a memoir published in the *Athenæum*, this was changed to 'Lutetiæ Parisiorum ad meliorem vitam abiit,' etc., which, Landor complained, would mean that she left Gore House for a better life at Paris.

We now come to Landor's correspondence with his friend Arthur de Noé Walker. More than sixty years ago an English boy, living with his family at Florence, made the acquaintance of Landor's sons. Going with a companion to see them at the Villa Gherardesca, they saw Landor himself, of whom, from the idle stories they had heard in Florence, they stood not a little in awe. And just as Emerson found none of the 'Achillean wrath and untameable petulance' he had been warned to expect, but the most patient and gentle of hosts, so the two English lads were pleasantly disillusioned. It was no choleric, unapproachable man of wrath who came out to greet them, but the true Landor who, as his manner was, gave them a right royal welcome, and insisted on their staying to dinner. 'How kind he is,' whispered one of the boys; and twenty years afterwards the other repeated the remark to Landor, who was delighted at the appreciation.

This was Arthur Walker's first meeting with
Landor, and shortly afterwards he went out to
India as a Company's Cadet, being presently
posted to the 6th Madras Infantry. It was
then that he was induced by a friend in the
Civil Service to read Landor's books ; and when
his regiment was quartered at Cuttack, he met
Landor's brother-in-law, at that time a captain
in the Bengal Artillery. Invalided during the
campaign in China, Captain Walker ' after hot
days in the wild wastes of war,' left the service
and came home.

Landor was now living in Bath, and Captain
Walker took the earliest opportunity of renew-
ing his acquaintance with one whom he had
since learnt to admire, not only as a genial
friend, but as a great writer. An inscription in
a copy of the two-volume edition of Landor's
works—'Walter Savage Landor, to his friend
Arthur Walker, Feb. 5, '47 '—commemorates
this second meeting. Thenceforward they met
frequently.

The earliest letter I have found is dated from
3, Rivers Street, Bath, and appears to have
been written in 1853. Landor alludes to the
beginnings of their friendship :

'I do not remember the first visit you made to me, but I well remember the last, hoping that it may not bear that name much longer. I think I must have owed to Arnold* the former, but the next will be the result of your kindness towards me.'

On leaving the Indian army, Captain Walker turned his attention to the study of medicine and surgery, and in 1854 he volunteered for service, as a surgeon, with the army in the Crimea. He arrived at the British camp a few days after the Battle of Inkermann.

   ' He call'd thee forth and led thee unapall'd
   Where Pestilence smote cities, vainly wall'd.
   May He who rules the tempest, O may He
   Protect and guide thee on the Euxine sea.'

So Landor wrote; and in another poem he refers to an incident during the attack on the Malakoff on June 18, 1855 :

        ' Thy strong shoulder bore
Amid the fiery sleet and heavier hail
The wretch whom Death lookt down on and past
   by.'†

---

* Arnold, Landor's eldest son, born 1818, died 1871.

† 'Heroic Idyls,' p. 115.

When the verses were published some years afterwards the printer 'took it into his head' to substitute 'freezing' for 'fiery.' 'Dear Arthur,' Landor wrote, 'evil genius has pursued me thro' life, and will soon bring me to its close. All my care about this cursed book has been in vain.' This letter, however, belongs to a later date. The following was written by Landor during the Crimean War:

To A. de N. Walker.

'Bath,
'*March* 3, [1856].

' Dear Arthur,

' Your letter dated 15 Feb. reached me this morning. It is so wise and humane that I could not resist my desire of sending it at once to the *Times*. Whatever you do does you honour, and the more because you have a higher motive. It is seldom that I myself have been able to perform any essential service to anyone. But it will please you to hear that I have procured a subscription for the descendant of Daniel Defoe by means of the *Times*.* Enough has been collected to make him comfortable for life. There is also a laboring man

---

* Landor's appeal on behalf of the descendants of Daniel Defoe was printed in the *Times* of November 5, 1855.

who writes wonderful poetry. For him also I have obtained subscribers, and have printed some dramatic scenes* for his benefit. This is all the little good I have been able to accomplish. Cappern's, the laborer's, poem on Balaclava I send enclosed. . . . Write to me again before you leave Balaclava, and tell me when I may probably see you. Meanwhile be sure how highly I esteem and love you.

'W. S. LANDOR.'

To A. de N. Walker.

'BATH,
'*Jan.* 12, 1857.

'DEAR ARTHUR,

'. . . Your campaign in the Krimea is infinitely more glorious than arms could have achieved. Welcome home again. Let me repeat these words to you in Bath ; and the sooner the better. You will find your old room and your old friend. . . .

'I read little now, chiefly *Punch* and the *Household*

---

* 'Antony and Octavius, Scenes for the Study,' by Walter Savage Landor. 'These scenes are dedicated to Edward Cappern, Poet and day-laborer, at Bideford, Devon. The dedication concludes with a Landorian outburst : 'Depend not on the favor of Royalty; expect nothing from it; for you are not a hound or a spaniel or a German prince.'

Words. I want amusing ideas, not serious ones.
. . . On the thirtieth* I enter my eighty-third
year.

' Ever affectionately yours,
' W. S. LANDOR.'

The remaining letters in this series were
written after Landor's return to Italy in 1858.
They mostly refer to the ' Heroic Idyls,' which
Dr. Walker, at his request, saw through the
press; but various other matters are touched
on which are of interest from the biographical
and bibliographical points of view.

To A. de N. Walker.

' FLORENCE,
' *Feb.* 23, [18] '60.

' DEAR ARTHUR,

' You shall certainly have a photograph of
me. . . . Here in Florence I have found several
men worth knowing; among the rest some
Americans. Winthrop, a member of Congress.
. . . Beside him, Story, son of the celebrated
jurist, Judge Story. You know the poetry of the
Brownings—most vigorous—she was Miss Barrett.
He is indefatigable in his good offices. . . .'

---

* January 30, 1857.

To A. de N. Walker.

'[FLORENCE,
'*July* 5, 1860.]

'DEAR ARTHUR,

'Your sister permits me to write a few lines at the back of her letter. I go to a villa a mile from Siena the day after to-morrow. You will find it pleasanter than Florence this hot weather. There will be a room kept for you. . . . Come soon. We can return to Florence time enough.

'Ever sincerely yours,
'W. S. LANDOR.'

The visit was duly paid, and Landor enlisted the services of his friend for the preparation and issue of another volume of poetry. In a letter dated December 2 (1860), he enclosed some verses, and promised to send more for the projected publication. 'So judicious a man as Mr. Newby,' he writes, 'will perhaps take the trouble to arrange the small pieces, both English and Latin, in the order in which it may be *supposed* they were written, some bearing the appearance of a young man, and others of an older.'

To A. de N. Walker.

'[FLORENCE,

'*Jan.*, 1861.]

'. . . I am now meditating an imaginary conversation between Virgil and Ovid (*sic*) on their journey to Brundusium. Do you know of any Periodical whose editor will give a few crowns for it to the subscription towards [? helping] the wounded under the command of Garibaldi? This composition I promise you shall not be worse than he generality of the others, altho' written in my eighty-seventh year, which will commence before the end of the present month. . . . I now read nothing but novels when I read at all, or turn back to Shakespeare.'

It was not Ovid with whom Virgil was to converse. In a letter, dated March 6, 1861, Landor wrote:

' DEAR ARTHUR,

' You are perfectly right in your remark that Ovid was only about 24 years old when Virgil *died*. But my conversation was between Virgil and Horace, not Ovid, who says, *Virgilium tantum vidi.* . . .'

The conversation duly appeared in the *Athenæum* on March 9, 1861, but Landor was vexed to find that there were mistakes in it.

For Ovid he would read Ovidius. 'We English say Ovid,' he remarked, 'but Romans say Ovidius. I have been careful in keeping the right names of the Antients.' Worse than this, three essential words had been omitted in an observation made by Horace. What Landor meant him to say to Virgil was: 'You have done wonders with a language so inflexible as ours, in which *the close of* almost every heroic verse is either a dissyllable or a trisyllable.' The three words in italics have yet to be inserted in a correct copy of the conversation.

A letter to Dr. Walker from his sister, the Contessa Baldelli, contains an interesting reference to Landor:

To A. de N. Walker.

'Florence,
'*March* 14, 1861.

'. . . . Mr. Landor has been very often here lately; and on his expressing a wish to go to the Protestant burial-ground here, I sent to propose driving him there. He happened to be rather sad, however, that morning, and said he would go this summer " before I am laid flat there." . . . The children had two peewits which they brought in to show him, and he nursed one in his arms for a long

time.   All at once he said: " This peewit will come
to an untimely end; I am sure of it."   " Why," I
replied, " what makes you think so ?"   " I feel
sure of it," he answered.   " I have been thinking
of it for the last two or three minutes." '

To A. de N. Walker.

'FLORENCE,
'*August,* 1861.

'. . . . It would be worth a scholar's while to
trace the different spellings of the same words from
Chaucer down to the present day.   Many are spelt
better by him than by any author since.   He avoids
the reduplication of vowels *ea*, etc., and ends the
word with *e*. . . .   The Elizabethan age, so highly
cried up, was the most corrupt of any, in language
as in morals.   Ben Jonson made a few good remarks
on some words.   For instance, he notices the
absurdity of writing *cannot*, uniting the two words,
and asks how you would decline its tenses. . . .
Middleton, whose Letter from Rome is a treasure
of higher value than even his life of Cicero, writes
taste and *haste* without the final vowel, which is
wrong and vulgar.   Our best writer now is Archbishop Whately.   In almost all the rest are
neologisms and slang. . . .   Horace Walpole was
a Frenchman in manners and conduct, but he wrote
pure English.   There may have been rouge on his
cheeks, but there was none in his writings.   He

wrote *red* when everybody else wrote and said *rouge.*
His Historical Doubts are very ingenious and admirably exprest. The family of Lucas in Glamorgan
has always been reputed to be descended from Perkin
Warbec. His tenants would have it that he was
the only man in the principality who was equal in
descent to Lord Dynevor.'

To A. de N. Walker.
'[FLORENCE,
'October, 1861.]

'DEAR ARTHUR,
'. . . . You will receive a case containing
two pictures—one is by Penni who worked with
Raffael, and is thought to contain the touches of this
master ; it is a copy, if not a duplicate of his larger
picture. This is *not* for you, but a rarer is—containing many figures by Mazzolina da Ferrara.
But take whichever you prefer, and forward the
other to the Rev. Mr. Tate, Widcombe, near Bath.
This gentleman had the kindness to keep a place
for me in that churchyard ; and, as he may soon
leave the parish, he thinks it advisable to have the
grave made and brickt directly. . . .'

To A. de N. Walker.
'[? FLORENCE,
'October, 1861.]

'DEAR ARTHUR,
'. . . . You are somewhat too indulgent to
Lytton. He writes worse lately. Hood's " Song

of the Shirt " is fairly worth all the poetry written since.   It sinks sadly deep in the sands of Germany. Are Gray and Goldsmith, are Cowper and Southey, are Keats and Shelley so utterly forgotten ? Bembo's epigram to Venice is the best thing in Latin verse between Ovid and Bobus Smith—but Bembo had imbibed faintly the spirit of poetry. His Latin, and Pico's di Mirandola, is excellent. . . .'

To A. de Noé Walker.

'FLORENCE,

'[1862].

'DEAR ARTHUR,

'During the last fortnight I have been incessantly occupied in writing and transcribing over and over again what I now send to you.   My poetry will find but little favour with the public, but I am confident that this will be red eagerly.   There is enough for a pamphlet of twenty or more pages. If Mr. Newby is so occupied that he cannot bring it out within the week after he receives it, throw it [away], for, like fish and venison, it must not stay on the table to get cold. . . .

'Ever affectionately yours,

'W. S. LANDOR.

'I hope to get some money by this—not for myself, as you shall see.'

From subsequent letters it appears that this pamphlet was entitled, ' Letters of a Canadian.'

Nothing of the kind is even mentioned in any of the lives of Landor; but though careful inquiries have failed to bring to light a single copy, there is no doubt that the letters were written and printed. Landor's name was omitted from the title-page, the pamphlet was still-born, and but for the correspondence now discovered, would most likely never have been heard of.

To A. de N. Walker.

'[FLORENCE,
' 1862.]

' DEAR ARTHUR,

' I had red the Laureate's Ode,* very spirited and poetical. But I discover a superfetation of rhymes—they are like the young frogs over the bodies of older. There are seven words that rhyme in the course of 13 lines. No ear can bear this buffeting. Rhymes are troublesome and capricious, sometimes holding back and sometimes coming un-called.

' It is difficult to keep them away from the higher poetry. Milton must have found it so occasionally.

---

* Tennyson's ' Ode on the Opening of the Great Exhibition.' This poem was published in *Fraser's Magazine*, June, 1862; but an unauthorized version had previously appeared in the *Times*.

. . . I wish our present poets would pay more attention to immovable and solid models, and less to
hollow and light plaster. The Laureate could well
afford to throw away the last verse of his Ode,
which, in fact, is two verses—an alexandrine in an
overall. Do not think I undervalue this excellent
man's poetry. He well deserves the station he
holds. . . .'

As usual, Landor was impatient at the delay
in printing his pamphlet. 'I am now anxious,'
he writes in an undated note, 'about the
" Letters of a Canadian." Send me three
copies of these, if they come into mouths which
are now agape and would soon be filled with
coarser stuff.' A note dated June 5 (1862) says :
' The Canadian letters came safe. Thanks
again.' In his next letter he says: ' Let
Monckton Milnes and Kenneth Mackenzie, 12,
Newton Road, have one, and Mrs. Linton,
Larrymore House, Hampstead.' He adds :

'I wish I never had anything to do with publishers. Duncan is the most honorable I have
found among them. My only anxiety in these
matters is that no incorrect copy of my last writings
may ever come before the world.'

To A. de N. Walker.

'[FLORENCE]
'*September* 11 [1862].

'. . . . Lately I have had one or two letters from America. Half the nation would utterly ruin the other half—would liberate the Blacks, who are well contented, and would enslave their masters under whom they were happy. Union is broken up for ever. Within half a century there will be fifty or more independent States:—Washington the capital of the Southern, New York of the Northern.'

To A. de N. Walker.

'[FLORENCE,
'1863].

'. . . . Above all things I am anxious that no copy of the book* be sent to me. God grant me patience to recover from what I have suffered already. The sight of anything relating to this accursed book might drive me distracted for another four days of the delirium it caused.

'Believe me ever, dear Arthur,
'Your affectionate old friend,
'W. LANDOR.'

---

* 'Heroic Idyls.'

To A. de N. Walker.

'[FLORENCE,
'1863].

'DEAR ARTHUR,

'A folded sheet is come leaving a blank between pp. 240 and 257. I am made to write (in note to 158 which is numbered wrong), endurated for indurated, p. 262, v. 13, spread for sprad, and p. 264, v. 7, Ptolemies for Ptolemais. God has preserved me from cutting my throat after this. . . . May you be happier than your affectionate

'W. L.'

CHAPTER V.

' There never was a right thing done, or a wise
one spoken, in vain.'

W. S. LANDOR.

A NUMBER of fragments in print, some of them
both rare and curious, were found in Landor's
desk. The earliest in date is a copy — un-
happily imperfect—of ' Poems from the Arabic
and Persian,' a thin quarto printed in 1800 by
Mr. Sharpe of Warwick. Wrapper, title-page,
and two pages of preface are needed to make
the volume complete; but what is left gains
additional value from the author's manuscript
corrections. These Arabic and Persian poems
—whether written in imitation of Asiatic verse,
or translated from a translation is uncertain—
were reprinted, but without the bulk of the
notes, in ' Dry Sticks ' (Edinburgh, 1858).

They cannot be found elsewhere; and the original edition—the thin quarto—of which only a hundred copies were printed for friends, is very scarce indeed. Mrs. Browning, who accepted Landor's assurance that he wrote these poems for the mystification of scholars, described them as extremely beautiful, breathing the true Oriental spirit throughout, 'ornate in fancy, graceful and full of unaffected tenderness.' Landor's annotations—as already said, they have all but dropped out of existence—are hardly less interesting than the text. Comparing Persian erotic verse with that of Greek and Latin authors, he says, with the felicity of decision which was the keynote of his style from the very first, 'Anacreon was the master, Tibullus the slave of Love; and while the Orientals are engaged in perplexing us, the Classics have seized his arrows and exercised a portion of his power.' In a letter of a later date, to Robert Southey, Landor said: 'I have read everything Oriental I could lay my hands on, and everything good may be comprised in thirty or forty lines. . . . I would rather have written the worst page in the Odyssea than all the stuff Sir William Jones makes such a pother and palaver on. . . . It is better to describe a girl getting a tumble over a skipping-rope made of a wreath of flowers.' After all, Landor did not differ so widely from Edward Fitzgerald, translator of Omar Khayyam's Rubaiyat, who, writing to Professor Cowell, said: 'O dear! when I look into Homer, Dante, and Virgil, Æschylus, Shakespeare, etc., those Orientals look—silly! Don't resent my saying so. *Don't* they?' I will quote the last of Landor's notes, printed after the lines 'To Rahdi.' The pretended translator says: 'This poem resembles not those ridiculous quibbles which the English in particular call Epigrams, but rather, abating some little for *Orientalism*, those exquisite *eidyllia*, those carvings, as it were, in ivory or gems, which are modestly called Epigrams by the Greeks.'

I have said that there is some uncertainty as to whether Landor invented these poems from the Arabic and Persian or translated them, as at first he professed to have done, from a French translation. The internal evidence can hardly be regarded as convincing either way. He ascribes the Arabic poems to the son of the Bedouin, Sheikh Dahir. Ahmed Dahir ruled over Acre from 1750 till 1776, when he was overthrown by Hassan Pacha and the soldier of fortune, Ahmed el Jezzar, who afterwards became celebrated for his defence of Acre against Bonaparte. According to the French traveller, M. Volney, Dahir had a son, Othman, who, 'on account of his extraordinary talents for poetry, was spared and carried to Constantinople.' Of this Othman, however, there is no further record. Moreover, according to some authorities, it was not Othman, but one Fazil Beg, a grandson of Ahmed Dahir, who was taken to Constantinople and became a poet; though whether there is anything in his extant writings which bears any resemblance to Landor's Arabic poems I cannot ascertain. With regard to the poems from the Persian, Professor E. G. Browne, of Cambridge, who most kindly gave me his opinion, inclines to the belief that they are not genuine translations. It might be worth while to reprint the poems, if only to find whether there is any means of arriving at a final decision as to their authenticity.

Of the printed papers in Landor's desk, next in order of date is his mutilated copy (with his name in autograph on the cover) of a volume published in 1802—'Poetry by the author of "Gebir."'   The missing portions are the title-page; pages 1 to 11, containing 'Chrysaor,' a narrative poem in blank verse, which made a deep impression on Wordsworth, and fore-shadowed, Mr. Colvin thinks, in subject and treatment the 'Hyperion' of Keats; and portions of pages 53 to 56.   Here again there is compensation in the shape of notes in the author's hand.   Of special significance are the additions made to another narrative poem, 'From the Phoceans.'   This was not reprinted either by Landor or Mr. Forster; and Mr. Colvin found it 'so fragmentary and obscure as to baffle the most tenacious student.'   Landor, writing to Robert Browning the year before his death, said: 'I am persuaded now that it is worth preserving as a curiosity of the kind;' but, years before, he admitted to Southey that it could never be expanded into a good poem. He had begun it, he then said, in a wrong key for English verse.   In Mrs. Browning's opinion 'From the Phoceans' took 'a high classic rank' along with 'Gebir.'

In a manuscript note which I have found among Landor's papers, he says:

'"Gebir" and "From the Phoceans" were written in the last century, when our young English heads were turned towards the French Revolution, and were deluded by a phantom of Liberty, as if the French could ever be free or let others be.'

'From the Phoceans' has been reprinted, without later emendations, in Mr. Crump's selections from Landor's poetry; but Mr. Crump was perhaps unaware of the fact that over three hundred verses, headed 'Part of Protis's narrative' (these he did not reprint) were a continuation of 'From the Phoceans,' and should have been reprinted with it. In another section of the present volume, I will give, from Landor's manuscript, a page or two of verse which was to have formed the conclusion of 'From the Phoceans.' More to show the extent of the additions in Landor's copy of the book than to remove the obscurity of the poem, I add here the lines that were to serve as a connecting link between the first part and the narrative of Protis:

' Here ended Hymneus: and the hall awhile
    Was silent, Arganthonius then arose.
    " My honored guests ! who bravely have endured
    The toils of exile and the storms of war,
    It will add little to your weariness,"
    Said he, " if ye will trace to us the ways
    By land and sea ye have gone thro', before
    Ye reacht the port wherein ye now shall rest."

' Then Protis, he who led them, thus replied :
    " O King ! the stranger finds in thee a friend
    Who found none in his kindred. But reproach
    Better becomes the weak than firmer breast.
    We will not turn to those who past us by
    In the dark hour : from such and from the land
    Where Pelops, in the days of heroes, reigned,
    We speed to Delphi : we consult the God, etc." '

At the end of Protis's narrative, Landor has
written :

' There would have been a second part of this
poem, narrating a sea-fight with the Carthaginians
recorded in history ; then conflicts with the natives.
The main difficulty was to devise names for them.
An approximation was attempted from the Welsh
and Irish, many of which are harmonious in the
termination, an essential in poetry.   Druids,
Druidesses, Bards, old oaks, and capacious wicker-
baskets were at hand.'

For the student's benefit another passage from Landor's letter to Browning may be quoted. 'At College,' he wrote, 'I and Stackhouse were examined by the college tutor in Justin, who mentions the expulsion of the Phoceans from their country. In my childish ambition, I fancied I could write an epic on it. Before the year's end I did what you see, and corrected it the year following.'*

I now come to a copy of a little work in prose, rarer, I think, than either of the volumes of poetry mentioned above. In the last year of his residence at Llanthony, Landor sent a series of letters on the state of European politics to the *Courier*. It was in the latter half of 1813, just after Bonaparte had been defeated at the battle of Leipzic. Southey, poet laureate, was composing the 'Triumphal Ode' to herald the new year, in which he proclaimed that

'Justice must go before,
And Retribution must make plain the way,
Force must be crushed by Force,
The power of evil by the power of good,
Ere order bless the suffering world once more,
Or peace return again.'

---

* Forster's 'Life of Landor,' i. 178.

' I, too,' Landor wrote to Southey, ' had been employing some midnight hours to prove that " Justice must go before "; but the evil genius to whom I committed the manuscript has printed what he chose and omitted the rest.' But before seeing what the letters contained, a word or two may be said on Landor's attitude toward politics at this particular period. He was the owner and occupier of a large landed estate, and he was also known, among men of letters of the first rank, as a writer of conspicuous genius, even though he displayed no faculty either of arresting the popular attention or of disarming the criticism that had broken the heart of Keats, and would have crushed, if it could, Wordsworth and Southey. With all his poetry and scholarship, his excursions in literature and love-making, there was much that seemed to mark him out, during the third decade of his life, as one who might take a leading part in directing the affairs of his country.   ' Had avarice or ambition guided me,' he wrote afterwards, ' remember I started with a larger hereditary estate than those of Pitt, Fox, Canning, and twenty more such amounted to. . . . My education and that which education works upon or produces was not below theirs.' It was Landor, the man of action, who, strange as it may seem to-day, once had thoughts of founding a kingdom in Crete—at least, I gather from one of Southey's letters* to him that he contemplated some such adventure. Certainly it was Landor, the man of action, who took up arms as a volunteer to help the Spaniards in their resistance to Bonaparte. Again, it was the resolute, energetic Landor who threw himself impetuously into the task of improving the Llanthony property. It was not the inditer of occasional epics and not occasional love-lyrics, nor was it a speculative philosopher, walking solitary on far eastern uplands, meditating and remembering, who addressed these letters to his countrymen on what was the burning topic of the day; but rather one who, so long as his home was in England, kept alert watch on all that involved the glory and welfare of his country; the interest he took therein being none the less real though he never ranked himself as a party man, and detested those who made politics a profession.

* Southey to Landor, May 2, 1808.

This reprint of the ' Letters of Calvus,' as the author entitled them, was meant, no doubt, for private circulation,* the portions omitted by the *Courier* being restored, and a fourteenth letter being added by way of postscript. Writing about them when they first appeared, Southey, in a letter to his brother, said :

' You have seen the letters in the *Courier* with the signature of CALVUS ?   Landor is the writer.   I entirely agree with him that this is the time for undoing the mischief done by the Peace of Utrecht. France was then made too strong for the repose of Europe, and she ought now to be stript of Alsace, Lorraine, and Franche-Comté.'

Since Mr. Forster merely makes passing reference to the letters, without quoting from them, a few extracts from what is probably the only unabridged copy in existence may not be unwelcome.   CALVUS addresses his remarks to Lord Liverpool and the Parliament.   He claims a right to be heard :

' I never wrote a pamphlet : I belong to no party, no faction, no club, no coterie ; I possess no seat in Parliament, by brevet or by purchase ; I can afford to live without it ; but I cannot afford that

---

* I know of no other copy of the reprint.

accumulation of taxes which will arise from another war, if after our experience we conclude another probationary peace, and enter on a new course of experiments with all our instruments unscrewed and all our phials evaporated.'

Then follows a brief statement of the author's proposals, in the shape of a series of questions intended to show that the time was opportune for destroying, once and for all, the offensive power of France, and putting an end to Bonaparte's ambition by compassing his execution or perpetual imprisonment. Is England, Landor asks, again to be contented with an experimental peace?

' Shall we fight only until he consents to exchange some stone walls for some sugar-plantations, and throws down the bag of horse beans that he holds up against our coffee? What scoffs, what bitter scorn would Lord Chatham have poured forth against England, crouching from an elevation to which she never rose before, down to a degradation to which the united world could not reduce her ! . . . "We are not to meddle," Lord Castlereagh says, " with that great and powerful country itself." Why not? Has not that great and powerful country meddled with every other? Is she not great and powerful because she has done so ?'

No war, says CALVUS, that is waged in vain can be glorious. Unless it brings an accession of power or freedom, blood will have flowed to no purpose. 'To engage in war with so futile a design as merely to bind at last an atheist with an oath, and an assassin with a piece of red tape, is as foolish and as wicked as to discharge a cannon into a crowded market-place for a jubilee.' The object of the war for which Landor's voice was raised was to be the extinction of Bonaparte; such being necessary for the repose and independence of Europe. Now was the fitting opportunity. Let the French, dejected, discomfited and scattered, recover their former power and posture, and England would never again come forward with the prowess and terrors now at her command:

'Your well-dressed ambassadors and your ingenious state-papers, in which I must observe that the weakest governments and the worst causes have generally shone most, may be very much admired in the drawing-room and at the breakfast-table, and you will have glorious opportunities of breeding up your children (I mean you who have seats in Parliament) to the study of diplomacy; but you will have lost for ever that bright pre-eminence on which you stand at present, and you must prepare the means of ·taxation for the support of indefinite and hopeless wars.'

Readers of to-day may find it hard to comprehend the feeling that inspired all this bellicosity. Landor's remarks on the respective merits of political parties in England will perhaps seem a trifle less antiquated :

' Whenever the Tories' (he wrote) 'have deviated from their tenets, they have enlarged their views and exceeded their promises. The Whigs have always taken an inverse course. Whenever they have come into power, they have previously been obliged to shift those maxims and to temporize with those duties, which they had not either the courage to follow or to renounce. The character of Lord Rockingham gave them a respectability, and the genius of Burke added a splendour, which have long since utterly passed away : and the nation sees at last that nothing is more unsound and perishable than what is founded on an oligarchy of gamesters and adventurers.'

But an appeal to party passion was remote from Landor's purpose. It was the nation he called upon to inflict condign punishment on 'the monster,' Bonaparte. 'Six months of active warfare, with all our heart and all our strength, will complete the task.' Here is another typical utterance :

'War, it has often been said, is a game of chance, in which governors are the players, and the things governed are the stakes. Bonaparte, with the consent and applause of all classes in France, played for the whole continent against his empire ; and every Frenchman took a share in the bank. After all sorts of packing and shuffling and tricking, to say nothing of mixing drugs of a soporific quality in the cakes and wine, he has lost all he played for. Yet we have such respect for his dexterity, such confidence in his honour, and such veneration for his goodness of heart, that we not only think of giving him back whatever he laid down, but also a great part of what he failed to win, and what, as belonging to others, we have no right to dispose of in any manner, without first obtaining their consent. Yet besides all this, we sweep the board for him, lift the candlesticks, and make him a present of the card-money.

'The English are the only people in the Universe that ever played voluntarily this losing game. They sit down to it quietly, night after night, to the astonishment of their observers, the despair of their friends, and the derision of their adversaries.'

There is much else in the ' Letters of Calvus ' one would like to quote, both in illustration of the writer's political opinions and also for the sake of those recurring flashes of insight and passages of the finest eloquence that are never long absent from Landor's pages. The exhortation so often heard in the 'Imaginary Conversations,' that a closer attention should be paid to the lessons of history, by those whose duty or ambition it is to manage the affairs of States, is insisted on in language not always at a pamphleteer's command. Kings and statesmen, CALVUS complains, will endure any insult rather than listen to those who entreat them to look to history for a guide. 'History would lead them into that chilly and awful chamber in which, under the suspended armour, they might read their own destinies.'

The fourteenth letter, to which Landor prefixed, in his own hand, the word 'Postscript,' is dated December 20, 1813. Since the preceding letters had been sent to the *Courier* he had perused the Manifesto of the Allied Powers. 'Who in the name of Heaven,' he asks, ' could have composed this flimsy tissue of folly, cowardice, and falsehood ?' But enough of the pamphlet has been quoted to show its nature, if not to gain for the letters of CALVUS a place in any collection of Landor's works that can be regarded as complete.

There remains to be noticed in this chapter a collection of shorter pieces, in prose and verse, of a later date. They are letters and poems sent by Landor, during his last residence in Bath, to the newspapers. With one or two unimportant exceptions, all the verses have been republished; but the letters will be new, except to the industrious bibliographer who has searched the files of the *Examiner* and the *Atlas*. The earliest is a letter on 'the comfortable state of Europe,' printed in the *Examiner* of September 8, 1849. Landor prophesied that there would be a great war in Europe before two years were out; and he was not far wrong. He was alarmed at the prospect of Russian aggression. 'Russia,' he wrote, 'is guided systematically by watchful and thoughtful, prompt and energetic ministers. Every step of hers is considerate and firm, is short and sure; she is exhausted by no hasty strides, she is enfeebled by no idle aspirations. France believes it to be her interest, and fancies it to be in her power to divide the world with her; and if two such nations with ambitions in accord are resolved on it, what power upon earth can effectually interpose?' Landor was no believer in dreams of universal peace. 'There never can be universal peace, nor even general peace long together, while three-score families stand forth on the high grounds of Europe, and command a hundred millions to pour out their blood and earnings whereon to float enormous bulks of empty dignities.'

In 1851, Landor was writing innumerable letters about Kossuth's visit to England. He had sold, or tried to sell, his pictures in order to raise money for the Hungarian revolt. When Kossuth sought a refuge in England, Landor organized a reception committee at Bath, and wrote a poem to be recited at a public meeting held in the patriot's honour at Birmingham. Kossuth at first seemed to resent Landor's impetuous enthusiasm, but ended by thanking him civilly enough for his efforts. Landor replied in a letter dated Bath, October 28, 1851:

'SIR,

'The chief glory of my life is that I was the first in subscribing for the assistance of the Hungarians at the commencement of their struggle.

The next is that I have received the approbation of their illustrious leader. I, who have held the hand of Kosciosko, now kiss with veneration the signature of Kossuth. No other man alive could confer an honour I would accept.

>   'Believe me, Sir,
>
>   'Ever yours most faithfully,
>
>   'WALTER SAVAGE LANDOR.'

About the same time, Landor sent the *Examiner* ten letters addressed to Cardinal Wiseman; but these have been reprinted in 'Last Fruit.' More interesting, however, and less accessible, are the letters he wrote during the Crimean War. The following protest against a form of intolerance, which is not without its counterpart in our own days, was printed in the *Atlas* of September 29, 1855:

>   'TO THE EDITOR OF THE *Atlas*.
> 'SIR,
>
>   'It is much to be regretted that the Christian religion, from the decease of the Apostles down to the present day, has produced more animosity and discord in the East than all the religions which it encountered and struggled to supersede. The star of Bethlehem was a morning star, appearing but too short a time above the horizon, and extending its radiance but a little

way beyond the circle it illuminated. I am led to these serious and sad reflections by seeing the Greek and Latin churches at daggers drawn still, after an incessant conflict for many centuries above a thousand years. All the religions in the world, innumerable as they have been and are, never shed so much innocent blood as that which arrogantly and falsely calls itself the Christian. The first lesson of its Divine teacher was goodwill toward all; but no sooner were the scholars out of school than they tore out that page, and scribbled un-intelligible words over the remainder of the volume. The ushers at last turned out the master, and declared he never knew what he had been talking about. It was their business, they said, to set him right; but he could not be set right until they had houses and lands to set him right in, with chains and padlocks for security. Story-tellers from the borders of the desert broke in among them as they were carousing, threw flask after flask upon the floor, called the people from round about, and told them a fresh series of equally marvellous and more pleasant stories. The candle, after flaring and glittering, went out; but left behind it, and still leaves, a close unwholesome stench.

' Recently there have been loud complaints against the followers of Mahomet for persecuting the Christians. I shall now examine this matter. Twelve years ago there appeared in the *Morning Chronicle* a refutation of a cruel judgment against an Armenian subject of the Ottoman Empire. This lies now before me. It was based on a statement made by the highest officer of State, whose name I do not feel myself at liberty to announce. This, however, I will venture to say of him: I wish we had in England a functionary of the same station possessing the same solidity of judgment and the same integrity.

'And now come forward fresh accusations against the most tolerant and indulgent government. It appears as if every priest and missionary were emulous of the Tzar. What portentous impudence is there in the Turkish Mission Aid Society, exprest as follows: "I am further directed by the committee most respectfully to submit to your lordship whether the present may not be a favourable juncture for the 'great community' represented at the Porte to urge on his Highness the Sultan that inasmuch as the pledge of March 21, 1844, appears to admit a different interpretation, and as doubts exist respecting its application to the case, his Highness may be pleased to make it so comprehensive as to include the exemption from the punishment of death, on account of religious offences, of all classes of his Highness's subjects." This is a requisition that blasphemy may go for nothing in Turkey, and a presumption that God can only be blasphemed in Anglo-Saxon. Will the clergy never be quiet? Will they never mind their own business, and their own laws, without an interference with foren

institutions ?   Did these noisy men who now appeal
to Lord Clarendon, as I read in to-day's newspaper,
ever raise a cry against Austria and Russia when
those Christian potentates drove Kossuth and the
other brave and virtuous defenders of their country
far away from it ?   Who at that hour of calamity
gave help and asylum to the lovers of their native
land, the defenders of their faith ?   Who, but the
most Christian of all Christian potentates, the
Khalif Abdul Medjid ?

'WALTER SAVAGE LANDOR.

'*September* 25.'

CHAPTER VI.

LANDOR AND HIS CONTEMPORARIES.

' We English are generally as fierce partizans in
literary as in Parliamentary elections, and we cheer
or jostle a candidate of whom we know nothing.'

W. S. LANDOR.

SOME of Landor's opinions on the work of his
fellow-labourers in ' letter-land ' have already
been brought to notice. It may not be altogether a vain undertaking to inquire more
closely what he thought about the writers of
his own time who, to use a phrase he liked,
made a noise in the world ; and also what they
in their turn thought of him. Such judgments,
of course, do not amount to a final decision in
either case. On the one hand, Landor's
sympathies and antipathies, where a contemporary was concerned, were not wholly
exempt from personal bias. That is a failing

which may often be observed in people who write books and read them; but somehow or other he is reckoned to have been specially liable to it. On the other hand, in regard to what his contemporaries said about him, posterity, as usual, will prefer to think for itself. A wiser generation consents to forget Mathias, 'the Pursuer of Literature,' and remembers Charles Lamb. It can cheerfully dispense with the 'Rosciad,' but it wants endless editions of Boswell. So we need not listen too earnestly to what Southey said about 'Gebir,' or to Landor's laudations of 'Kehama.' Still it is a fact of some significance that many, if not all, the foremost English authors of the nineteenth century have agreed in recognizing his power. Southey, Wordsworth, Coleridge, Byron, and Shelley, as well as Dickens, Browning, and Swinburne, have confessed his greatness. As for his opinions on his coevals, if at times they are too laudatory, it rarely happens that they err in the other direction. Edward Fitzgerald said that Landor seemed to judge of books and men as he did of pictures, 'with a most uncompromising perversity, which the phrenologists must explain to us after his death.'* But this was in conversation, when Landor's extravagance of enthusiasm always became more boisterous and more pronounced. In writing, he very seldom lays down a criticism which is altogether perverse; while, as a general rule, his literary judgments, on ancients and moderns alike, bear the unmistakable stamp of sound taste, extensive knowledge both of books and men, and matured reflexion.

Wordsworth, Scott, Coleridge, Southey, and Lamb all came into the world about the same time as Landor. De Quincey and Byron, Shelley and Keats, were a little later. He was a man of five-and-twenty when Macaulay was born. Tennyson, Thackeray, Mr. Gladstone, Charles Dickens, and Robert Browning were all born during the third decade of his life. Of his immediate contemporaries, it was Robert Southey who had most influence over him. To Southey he owed the first public acclamation of his talents; Southey writing in the *Critical Review* that he had read ' Gebir ' repeatedly ' with more than common attention, and with far more than common delight.' That

* Fitzgerald to F. Tennyson, May 7, 1854.

was the foundation of a friendship, of the warmest kind, which lasted for forty years, unbroken by a single misunderstanding. 'The Curse of Kehama' and 'Thalaba the Destroyer,' and even 'Roderick,' have gone out of fashion nowadays ; and Landor's estimate of Southey's poetry would be thought too exalted. These three poems, he said, surpassed any three of Wordsworth's, who wanted Southey's diversity and invention as well as his humour. And yet it was the man, rather than his writings, that Landor more especially admired. 'If his elegant prose and harmonious verse are insufficient to incite enthusiasm, turn to his virtues, to the ardour and constancy of his friendships, to his disinterestedness, to his generosity.' There, at any rate, Landor stands on safe ground. Southey also valued Landor more highly as a friend than as a maker of books. 'Never did man,' he said, 'represent himself in his writings so much less generous, less just, less compassionate, less noble in all respects than he really is. I certainly never knew anyone of brighter genius or of kinder heart.'

With Wordsworth Landor was not always in

touch.   At first, and when Wordsworth's merits were eclipsed by the popularity of Byron, Landor was loud in his praise.   ' In thoughts, feelings, and images not one amongst the antients equals him, and his language (a rare thing) is English.'*   No poet since Milton, he makes Southey say, had exerted greater powers with less of strain and less of ostentation.   ' Laodamia ' was ' a composition such as Sophocles might have exulted to own.'   This admiration was repaid in kind.   ' It could not but be grateful to me,' Wordsworth wrote, ' to be praised by a poet who has written verses of which I would rather have been the author than of any produced in our time ; and what I now write to you I have frequently said to many.'   The verses referred to were ' Gebir ' and ' Count Julian.'

But Landor's liking for Wordsworth, as they grew older, underwent diminution.   At a breakfast party, where both were present, Wordsworth said, or Landor fancied he said, that he would not give five shillings for all Southey's poetry.   ' My spirit,' Landor afterwards wrote, ' rose against his ingratitude toward the man

* Landor to Southey, 1818.

who first, and with incessant effort and great difficulty, brought him into notice.'*   In a second conversation between Southey and Porson, published originally in *Blackwood's Magazine*,† Landor's disapproval of what he held to be flaws in Wordsworth's poetry was put in a shape that could hardly fail to vex and grieve the future Laureate's admirers.   Porson is made to say that ' among all the bran in the little bins of Mr. Wordsworth's beer-cellar there is not a legal quart of that stout old English beverage with which the good Bishop of Dromore regaled us.'   The insinuation is not outrageously unfair.   After a course of ' Chevy Chase ' and ' Otterburne ' a good many people might find even the ' Excursion ' a trifle flat. Nor is Porson so very wide of the mark when he says that Wordsworth's is an instrument which has no trumpet-stop.   Descending to particulars, he lays his finger on inanities which even a devout Wordsworthian must deplore.   Landor also makes Porson the vehicle for some parodies of Wordsworth. One of them begins :

* ' Letter to Emerson.'

† December, 1842.

I.

' Hetty, old Dinah Mitchell's daughter,
　　Had left the side of Derwentwater
　　　About the end of Summer.
I went to see her at her cot,
　Her and her mother, who were not
　　　Expecting a new comer.

II.

' They both were standing at one tub,
　You might have heard their knuckles rub
　　　The hempen sheet they wash'd.
The mother suddenly turn'd round,
　The daughter cast upon the ground
　　　Her eyes, like one abasht.'

And so on. The whole tone of Porson's remarks rather suggests that Landor regretted having praised Wordsworth so highly in former conversations.

However this may be, it served to make Wordsworth's son-in-law, Edward Quillinan, exceedingly angry. Four months later there appeared in *Blackwood's* an Imaginary Conversation written by Mr. Quillinan, who referred, in a note, to Landor as a garrulous sexagenarian. Landor possibly would have pocketed this affront had not a charge of plagiarism been added thereto; of plagiarism, moreover, from the very writer who, as the garrulous sexagenarian was never tired of re-iterating, had stolen a sea shell from 'Gebir.' Landor had made Southey say: 'Wit appears to require a certain degree of unsteadiness in the character. Diamonds sparkle the most brilliantly on heads stricken by the palsy.' Now Wordsworth, in a little poem written in 1818, and called 'Inscriptions in a Hermit's Cell,' had said:

> 'Diamonds dart their brightest lustre
> From a palsy-shaken head.'

The resemblance was indisputable, but Landor never told his mortification. He only hastened to cancel the passage; and when the dialogue was reprinted in 1846, not only had all traces of the plagiarism disappeared, but some of Porson's sharpest criticisms, together with the parody quoted above, had been cut out.

It is Mr. Forster who tells us that Sir Walter Scott found much to admire in 'Gebir,' having read the poem on Southey's commendation. According to the same authority, Landor fancied that Scott's appreciation was shown by borrowing from 'Gebir' without acknowledgment; and Mr. Forster found a list of the alleged peculations in Landor's hand. Landor never quite forgave Sir Walter Scott either for this or for his loyal attentions to the Prince Regent; but it did not prevent his expressing, in the highest terms, his regard for Scott's merits as a writer whether in prose or verse. 'The trumpet blast of Marmion' delighted him. No large poem of the time, not even Southey's 'Roderick' was so animated, or so truly heroic. The battle scene, he declared, was one of the four epic pieces transcending all others; the other three being the colloquy of Achilles and Priam in Homer's 'Iliad,' the contention of Ulysses and Ajax in Ovid's 'Metamorphoses,' and the first book of Milton's 'Paradise Lost.' He was no less ready to praise the Waverley Novels. At first, the 'Heart of Midlothian' was his favourite; but in his old age, it was 'Kenilworth' that he liked best. There is a freshness in all Scott's scenery, he makes Porson say to Southey, and a vigour and distinction in all his characters. 'He seems the brother in arms of Froissart,' and it would not be easy to hit on a happier comparison. He also puts into Porson's mouth a wicked story about Wordsworth, who, being invited to read one of the Waverley Novels, and finding at the commencement a quotation from his own poetry, totally forgot the novel, and recited the poem from end to end, with many comments and more commendations. No doubt there are some people who will laugh at Landor for ranking Scott above Byron as a poet; but a good deal might be said in favour of his choice, and he was always ready to vindicate it.

In one of his letters to his sister, Landor told her of a visit he paid to Samuel Taylor Coleridge at Highgate, in 1832. Coleridge would not come downstairs till he had arrayed himself in the sumptuous splendour of a brand new suit of black, brought out in honour of the occasion. When at length he appeared, he welcomed his visitor with 'as many fine speeches as he could ever have made to a pretty girl'; though that sort of eloquence, may be, was less in Coleridge's line than Landor's. Possibly it was at the same solemn interview that, after quoting fourteen German poets of the first rank, Coleridge expressed his compassion for Æschylus and Homer, which is one of Landor's stories about him. The new suit of broadcloth was no doubt the outward and visible sign of a real regard for Landor's character and genius. Not that Coleridge rated Landor with first-class writers. A couple of years after this visit, he delivered himself of the following judgment:

'What is it that Mr. Landor wants, to make him a poet? His powers are certainly very considerable, but he seems to be totally deficient in that modifying faculty which compresses several units into one whole. . . . His poems, taken as a whole, are unintelligible; you have eminences excessively bright, and all the ground around and between them is darkness. Besides which, he has never learned, with all his energy, to write simple and lucid English.'*

A raking criticism of that kind, however, is ineffective without examples, which Coleridge does not venture on. It is otherwise when Landor criticizes Coleridge. For instance, in a letter to Mr. Forster, after admitting that few men in our time have written more eloquently than Coleridge, he adds: 'But to say things

* 'Table Talk,' January 1, 1834.

well is not enough for wisdom,' and he quotes from 'Lay Sermons' what Coleridge said in favour of reviving 'the ancient feeling of rank and ancestry as a counterbalance to the commercial spirit now prevalent.' 'What,' Landor asks, 'could be more contrary to the spirit of Christianity, or indeed more absurd in itself; for how extremely small a number can possibly be actuated by the antient feeling of rank and ancestry?' Landor himself was by no means inclined to forego his own pride of descent. In spite, however, of all that has been said to the contrary, he cared little about other people's ancestors. The religious argument may surprise the reader; but the truth is that Landor was never an irreligious man. He did not like priestcraft, and made no mystery of his feelings on that score. Yet he was far from being an agnostic. In his 'Letters of an American'—a little book one seldom meets with — the supposed writer, Jonas Pottinger, says : ' I hope to be always a Christian, never a theologian'; and he adds in true Landorian style: 'There are things which I believe, things which I disbelieve, things which I doubt. Among the latter is this, that I can ever be carried to heaven on the shoulders of a cod-fish, or get forward a good part of the journey on a smooth and level road, on a couple of eggs for rollers.'

It might be mentioned here that the late Chief Justice, Lord Coleridge, was among Landor's constant readers, and what is more remarkable, he has convicted him of a misquotation from the Latin. The autograph of 'John Duke Coleridge,' with the date 1853, is on the fly-leaf of my copy of 'Last Fruit off an old Tree,' published in that year; and on page 305 there is a marginal note in the same handwriting. Landor had said:

'How beautifully does Ovid, who is thought in general to have been less tender, and was probably less chaste [than Petrarch], refer to the purer objects of his affection !—
' " Unica nata, mei justissima causa doloris," etc.

The marginal note says, rightly enough :

' This is not Ovid; it is Propertius,* and the line in the original is somewhat different. *Nata* does not mean *daughter* in the context, and the mistake is curious for an accurate scholar like Landor.'

Landor and Lord Byron were not formed for

* Propertius, ii., xxv. 1.

mutual admiration. Still, they might have said nothing uncivil of each other had it not been for Landor's offensive and defensive alliance with Southey. When the opening cantos of 'Don Juan' appeared, Southey, in a preface to his 'Vision of Judgment,' entered an angry protest against the wickedness and immodesty of the Satanic school, quoting in support of his animadversions a passage from Landor's 'De cultu atque usu Latini sermonis.' Then a report got abroad in literary circles that Landor had said he would not or could not read Byron's poems ; and it may even be surmised that some verses of Landor's on Byron's marriage had obtained the same currency. They were not published till 1831, and are not reprinted in Mr. Forster's editions, so there is an excuse for quotation :

> ' Weep, Venus, and ye
> Adorable Three
> Who Venus for ever environ !
> Pounds, shillings, and pence
> And shrewd sober sense
> Have clapt the strait waistcoat on * * *
> Off, Mainot and Turk,
> With pistol and dirk,

> Nor palace nor pinnace set fire on :
> The cord's fatal jerk
> Has done its last work,
> And the noose is now slipt upon * * *'

To Southey, Byron replied in another 'Vision of Judgment,' praised by Leigh Hunt as the most masterly satire since Pope. In the preface Landor was referred to as one 'who cultivates much private renown in the shape of Latin verses.' There is an allusion also to 'Gebir,' 'wherein,' said Byron, 'the aforesaid Savage Landor (for such is his grim cognomen) putteth into the infernal regions no less a person than the hero of his friend, Mr. Southey's heaven—yea, even George the Third.' A year later (1823) Byron found another opportunity for a hit at Landor, whom, in a note to 'the Island,' he named as the author of Latin poems ' which vie with Martial and Catullus ' in what is least admirable. Lastly, in the eleventh canto of ' Don Juan,' published in August of the same year, came the lines so often quoted when Landor is mentioned by people who do not take the trouble to read him :

> ' That deep-mouth'd Bœotian, Savage Landor,
> Has taken for a swan rogue Southey's gander.'

In private Byron would express his admiration of Landor's generosity and independence, of his profound erudition and brilliant talents. Such concessions, however, were unlikely to disarm a man of Landor's temper. In the Imaginary Conversation between Bishop Burnet and Humphrey Hardcastle, Byron is referred to as George Nelly, reputed son of Lord Rochester. ' Whenever he wrote a bad poem, he supported his sinking fame by some signal act of profligacy —an elegy by a seduction, a heroic by an adultery, a tragedy by a divorce.' Nor was a saving clause without its sting. ' Say what you will of him, once whispered a friend of mine, there are things in him strong as poison and original as sin.'

The passage had hardly been printed when news came of Byron's death at Missolonghi. Landor was profoundly touched. In a note inserted in the second edition (1826) of the volume containing the conversation, he wrote :

' Little did I imagine that the extraordinary man, the worst of whose character is here represented, should indeed have been carried to the tomb so prematurely. If before this dialogue was printed he had performed those services to Greece which will render his name illustrious to eternity . . . the performance of which I envy him from my soul, and as much as any other does the gifts of heaven he threw away so carelessly, never would I, from whatever provocation, have written a syllable against him.'

Landor seems to have shared his mother's estimate of Byron, whose high abilities, that lady said, ' had given him the power of doing much good, which he failed to do.' Eleven years before, Byron had written in his private journal: ' The most I can hope is that someone will say—he might, perhaps, if he would.'

As time went on, Landor's dislike, both of Byron and of much that he wrote, became more and more emphatic. Allowing him to be the keenest and most imaginative of satirists, Landor saw less to admire in ' the Oriental train and puffy turban,' only put on, he suggested, in order to attract feminine notice, and perfumed with a superabundance of musk. That is a fairer hit than the accusation which Byron brought against Landor. Nor was the ' Bœotian ' far wrong when he said that Byron lacks the freshness and sanity that delight us in Burns ; or again when he compares the author of ' Lara ' and the 'Corsair' to a horse that has good action but tires by fretting and tossing his head and rearing. In his own occasional verse Landor would often launch out in dispraise of Byron :

> 'Say, Byron, why is thy attar
> Profusely dasht with vinegar ?'

In some verses addressed to 'The Recruits of Poetry,' he exhorts them to leave in the rear

> 'Asthmatic Wordsworth, Byron piping hot,'

and to march with 'manly Scott.' For 'Marmion'—'at first too much applauded, now too much underrated'—always pleased Landor better than 'Byron's trash.' But while he detested 'Giaours' and 'Corsairs,' he could praise Byron's 'Dream'; a poem, he said, that will always live. The *Quarterly Review*, years ago, charged Landor with speaking of Byron as a mere rhymer, wholly devoid of wit or genius. Landor's answer was that he had done nothing of the kind; he was ready to admit that Byron possessed much of both qualities, 'not always well applied.' And it was of Byron he spoke when he said that 'an indomitable fire of poetry, the more vivid for the gloom about it, bursts through crusts and crevices of an unsound and hollow mind.'

If one wished to show how widely Landor and Byron stood apart from each other in their way of looking at things, no more striking instance could be given of their incompatibility of judgment than is contained in what each said about Keats. Byron talked of the drivelling idiotism of the poet who had already written his ' Endymion ' and the 'Ode on a Grecian Urn.' Some of the expressions he used, though they are scarcely veiled even in the latest editions of Moore's 'Life of Lord Byron,' are unfit for publication. Almost worse is the coarse malignity which prompted Byron, in a letter to Mr. Murray, to say, ' No more of Keats, I entreat—flay him alive ; if some of you don't, I must do it myself.' Afterwards, indeed, when poor Keats was in his grave, Byron declared that he did not envy the man who had written the murderous article in the *Quarterly ;* but he nevertheless thought the affair a proper subject for an ill-natured jest. Which would one rather have written, Byron's doggerel, ' Who killed John Keats ?' or Landor's verse :

' Fair and free soul of poesy, O Keats !
  O how my temples throb, my heart-blood beats,
    At every image, every word of thine !
  Thy bosom, pierced by Envy, drops to rest ;
  Nor hearest thou the friendlier voice, nor seest
    The sun of fancy climb along thy line.'*

Landor, who was living in Italy when Keats came there to die, regretted afterwards that they had never met. One would like to think that Keats was praised during his lifetime by Landor ; but this seems doubtful. In a letter to Southey, written in 1825, there is mention of the 'sycophantic ruffian' who had recommended the author of ' Endymion ' to go back to his gallipots. A year or two later, in a letter to his sister Elizabeth, Landor said : ' By the way, you have not read Keats and Shelley ; *read them*.' I do not know, however, of any earlier allusion to Keats ; and Keats was now **dead.** But **thenceforward** Landor's admiration found frequent utterance. Keats, he said, was the most imaginative of English poets, after Chaucer, Spenser, Shakespeare, and Milton. There might be wild thoughts in his poetry and extravagant expressions ; 'but in none of

* ' Imaginary Conversations,' 1828, iii. 427.

our poets, with the sole exception of Shakespeare, do we find so many phrases so happy in their boldness.'* Landor, however, found fault with Shelley's remark that Keats was truly a Greek, which was Shelley's way of accounting for the fact that the author of 'Hyperion' could not read a line of Homer in the original. 'Between you and me,' Landor wrote, 'the style of Keats is extremely far removed from the very boundaries of Greece.'

In one of the Imaginary Conversations in which Landor speaks in his own person, he protests that if ever again he visits Rome, it will be to spend an hour, in solitude, where the pyramid of Cestius points to the humbler tombs of Keats and Shelley. He had never met Shelley; for when they were both living at Pisa, someone had told him a story about the younger poet, which Landor thought so disagreeable, that he avoided him. It turned out to have been untrue. 'I blush in anguish,' Landor then wrote, 'at my prejudice and injustice;' and whenever he spoke of Shelley afterwards, he would praise him both for his

* Works, 1846, i. 339. The passage quoted does not appear in the 1876 edition.

virtues and for his writings, and as one who united the ardour of the poet with the patience and virtue of the philosopher. 'Shelley,' he said, 'may have had less vigour than Byron, and less command of language than Keats;' but he himself would rather have written his—

> ' Music, when soft voices die,
>   Vibrates in the memory '

than all the lyrics of the Elizabethans, Shakespeare's only excepted. Elsewhere he says that Shelley and Keats were inspired with a stronger spirit of poetry than any other writer since Milton, Robert Burns only excepted.* 'I sometimes think,' he added, 'that Elizabeth Barrett Browning comes next'; an opinion which not many people would have endorsed forty years ago.

Neither Shelley nor Keats lived long enough to judge Landor by his most finished work; but the former, at any rate, needed no further evidence of his poetic power than was displayed in his very earliest books. Shelley, when he was at Oxford, was always reading 'Gebir, either to himself or aloud to his friends, who

* Letter to Mr. Forster, April 26, 1858.

were not always tolerant of his infatuation. One of them, eager to tell him something of importance and finding him immersed in the volume, threw it out of the window; but it was brought indoors again, and in a few minutes Shelley was as deep as ever in the woes of the Gadite king.

But while recalling what Landor and some of his brother poets of the first half of the century said of each other, we ought not to overlook a writer of prose who, like Landor, also rhymed on occasions. Charles Lamb was born only a few weeks after Landor; and, unlike as they were in some respects, they also had much in common. To the superficial observer, perhaps, no two men would have seemed less akin than the shy, gentle Elia, quietly eking out his little pittance from the East India House by unobtrusive contributions to the periodicals of the day, and the confident, large-voiced country gentleman, who could squander in a few months as much as Lamb earned in as many years, and who grandly professed to despise the emoluments of literature. How would it have been with them, one is tempted to ask, had Lamb inherited a fortune and had

Landor been forced to dip his daily bread in ink
and to work for a living ? Yet if destiny not
only led them along widely different paths of
life, but also brought out qualities and capacities
in the one altogether unlike those to which it
allowed free play in the other, and if there were
unmistakable divergencies of temper, intellect,
and attainments, each alike had a genius and
style of his own ; each in literature pursued the
same ideal, so far as mere writing goes ; each,
when his own taste and conscience were satisfied,
cared nothing for the disapproval, and little for
the applause, either of a coterie or of the crowd.
So it is not strange that Charles Lamb and
Walter Landor knew each other for kindred
spirits. The recognition seems first to have
come from Lamb. Describing his memorable
voyage in the old Margate Hoy, Lamb quotes a
line from ' Gebir ' :

' Is this the mighty ocean ?   Is this all ?'

Doubtless, too, when he talked about the sweet
security of London streets, a passage in ' Count
Julian '* was running in his head. When Southey
sent him a presentation copy of ' Roderick,'

* ' Count Julian : a Tragedy,' Act ii., Scene 5.

Lamb said he must read Landor's 'Julian' again. He could only recollect fine-sounding passages, and was inclined to think that Landor had failed in some of the characters. However, his memory, he confessed, was weak, and he would not by trusting to it ' wrong a fine poem.' A few years later, and after Lamb's gaol delivery from the bondage of the India House, we have evidence that he read the ' Imaginary Conversations.'   In one of the earliest of them Landor had started the odd theory that ' Don Quixote ' was nothing more nor less than a dexterous attack on the worship of the Virgin Mary.   Cervantes, he makes President du Paty say, was never such a knight errant as to attack knight errantry—a folly, if it was one, which had disappeared a century before.   Don Quixote was the Emperor Charles V., ' devoting his labours and vigils, his wars and treaties, to the chimerical idea of making minds, like watches, turn their indexes, by a simultaneous movement, to one point ' ; while Sancho Panza symbolized the people, sensible in other matters, but ready to follow the most extravagant visionary in this.   The notion did not commend itself to Charles Lamb, who protested against ' Landor's unfeeling allegorizing away of honest Quixote.'* Landor, he declared, might as well say that Strap, in Smollett's ' Roderick Random,' was meant to symbolize the Scottish nation before the Union, and Random the same nation after; or that Fielding's Partridge stood for the mystical man, and Lady Bellaston for the ' woman upon many waters.' For all Lamb knew to the contrary, ' Gebir ' might mean the state of the hop market a month ago. Landor, more likely than not, never heard of Lamb's objection to his gloss on Don Quixote; but when a *Quarterly Reviewer* in 1837 cited the same theory as a notable instance of Landorian whim, he took some pains to elaborate this part of the conversation.

Landor's liking for Lamb was unqualified. Writing to Henry Crabb Robinson in April, 1831, he quoted a sentence or two from ' Mrs. Leicester's School,' and went on to say : ' If your Germans can show us anything comparable to what I have transcribed, I would almost undergo a year's gurgle of their language for it.' In another letter of the same year he declared that Elia's essays in the *New Monthly Magazine*

* Letter to Mr. Southey, August 19, 1825.

were admirable—'the language truly English.
We have none better, new or old.' In the
following year Landor, revisiting England,
called on the Lambs at Enfield. Crabb Robinson was of the party, and describes the visit.
Lamb and his sister, one can imagine, may
have been a little embarrassed by the large
utterance and expansive manner of their new
friend. 'I thought Lamb by no means at his
ease,' Crabb Robinson tells us, 'and Miss Lamb
was quite silent.' Landor, however, was delighted with them both, as also with Miss Isola,
for whose album he presently wrote some verses.
It was his only meeting with Charles Lamb :

' Once, and once only, have I seen thy face,
    Elia !   Once only has thy tripping tongue
Run o'er my breast, yet never has been left
Impression on it stronger or more sweet.
Cordial old man ! what youth was in thy years !'

These lines were written on receiving the
news of Lamb's death, when, also, to the
sister of Elia Landor addressed the well-known
verses beginning :

' Comfort thee, O thou mourner, yet awhile !
        Again shall Elia's smile
        Refresh thy heart.'

Both poems have been reprinted, but a letter of Landor's, published in Leigh Hunt's *London Journal*,* is not to be found in his collected works. 'The Essays of Elia,' he said, 'will afford a greater portion of pure delight to the intellectual and the virtuous, to all who look into the human heart, for what is good and graceful in it, than any other two prose volumes, modern or ancient.'

There is not much that can profitably be added to what Landor says, in the extracts that have been given from his private letters, about the later generation of English writers who began to flourish when he was an old man. Browning dedicated a volume of poetry to him, and came to his rescue in those dark days when he was a homeless wanderer in Florence. Landor had been among the first to welcome Browning as a great poet—'A very great poet,' he wrote in 1845, 'as the world will have to agree with us in thinking.' He only wished that Browning would 'atticize' a little. 'Few of the Athenians had such a quarry on their property, but they constructed better roads for the conveyance of the material.' And Mrs.

* July 11, 1835.

Ritchie, in her delightful reminiscences, has told us how Browning would take down one of Landor's many books that stood on the book-shelves, and vow that he knew of no better reading. Nor had Landor been less ready to single out Tennyson from the band of minor poets who were trying their wings in the early days of the Victorian era.

In 1837 a volume of poetry* for the drawing-room table was published by subscription, her Majesty the Queen heading the list of subscribers. Among those who contributed were Southey, Wordsworth, Tom Moore, James Montgomery, Henry Taylor, Monckton Milnes, the Tennysons, and Landor himself. Alfred Tennyson sent the stanzas :

> 'Oh! that 'twere possible
> After long grief and pain,' etc.,

which afterwards, with alterations, became part of 'Maud.' In that same year Landor was shown a manuscript poem by Tennyson, which he at once pronounced to be Homeric, rivalling

* 'The Tribute.'

some of the finest passages in the 'Odyssey.'
It was the 'Morte d'Arthur.' Six years later
Landor was delighted with 'Ulysses' and
'Godiva,' liking the last-named poem, perhaps,
all the better because he himself had written
verses about Godiva when he was a schoolboy at Rugby. And when the finished version of 'Maud' came out, Tennyson rose yet
higher in his estimation. What other modern
poet, he asked, could have written the verse
in the 'Ballad of Oriana,' worth whole
volumes—

'O breaking heart that will not break'!

Everyone knows, of course, that Landor and
Dickens were close friends, and that Landor
is Mr. Boythorn in 'Bleak House.' Landor's
liking for Dickens found expression in two or
three of his poems, and in the dedication of the
volume in which he collected his Greek and
Roman Conversations. Possibly he did not
think quite so highly of Thackeray, but he called
'Esmond' a noble story, and the 'Lectures on
the Four Georges' were very much to his
taste. Someone has written on the fly-leaf
of my first edition of the 'Imaginary Con-

versations' the following verses which, he says, Landor recited *ex tempore* for Thackeray's edification when he met him after the delivery of the lectures:

' I sing the Georges four,
For Providence could stand no more.
Some say that far the worst
Of all the four was George the First ;
But still by some 'tis reckon'd
That worser still was George the Second.
No mortal ever said one word,
Or good or bad of George the Third.
When George the Fourth from earth descended,
Thank Heaven ! this line of Georges ended.'

A distinguished critic* has expressed his astonishment that Thackeray was seldom, ' if ever,' mentioned by Landor. They moved in different planes, but Landor would have been the last man to affect indifference to the merits of a contemporary.

Mr. Forster's biography fitly ends with the memorial verses written by Mr. Swinburne, who, a few months before Landor died, went to Florence on purpose to see him—

* Professor Saintsbury.

> ' The youngest to the oldest singer
>   That England bore.
>
> I found him whom I shall not find
>   Till all grief end,
> In holiest age our mightiest mind,
>   Father and friend.

To this felicitous determination of Landor's place among English writers of the nineteenth century, one may well hesitate to add so much as a single word.

CHAPTER VII.

UNPUBLISHED VERSE.

' Poetry was ever my amusement; prose my
study and business.'

W. S. Landor.

A number of miscellaneous poems by Landor,
all of them found among the papers in his
writing-desk, have now to be given. For reasons
already stated, it has not been considered necessary to print the whole collection ; but an endeavour has been made to rescue as much as
seemed worth preserving. Only in a few cases
has a heading been supplied by Landor ; nor
was it possible to discover his wishes as to the
order in which the poems should appear. A
few explanatory notes have been added. First
come a number of poems which should have a
place among those quoted or referred to in the
chapter on Landor's loves and friendships.

Then follow verses embodying his views on various points of philosophy, politics and literature, together with a few others which are mainly of interest for the light they may throw on his life and character.

WRITTEN IN 1793.

'TELL me what means that sigh,' Ione said,
When on her shoulder I reclined my head;
And I could only tell her that it meant
The sigh that swells the bosom with content.

THE FEARFUL (1801).*

I would not see thee weep but there are hours
  When smiles may be less beautiful than tears,
Some of those smiles, some of those tears were
    ours;
Ah! why should either now give place to fears?

* This and the preceding poem have a particular interest, as they are dated by Landor himself. In 1801 he narrowly escaped marrying a rich heiress; 'but after committing a piece of foolery, in which I was the puppet, the farce ended.' The date ascribed to the verse in which Ione is named was that of his first year at Oxford. His biographers, however, have supposed that he met Ione in 1795.

ABERTAWY.*

Along the seaboard sands there grows
The tiniest and the thorniest rose,
And tawny snapdragons stand round,
Above it, on the level ground.
' Here,' said I, ' sit, or you will weary
Before you come to Briton Ferry.'
And I began to pluck away
The stubborn twisting roots.

                        ' Stay ! stay !'
She cried ; ' your hand begins to bleed.'
I hid it ; for it bled indeed.
' Now do not hold it back,' said she,
' No, nor deny it ; let me see.'
With gentle violence she prevail'd,
For when has gentle violence fail'd?
How sat we down ? who smooth'd the
    sand ?
Who cured, and how was cured, that hand?
It was a dream ; which to explain
I try (and so will you) in vain.

---

* These lines, probably an earlier version of a little poem published in ' Heroic Idyls,' p. 157, and reprinted in the Works, 1876, viii., 320, undoubtedly commemorate a walk with Miss Rose Aylmer.

TO ROSE.

WITH A PORTRAIT OF PETRARCH'S LAURA.*

In her green vest and golden hair,
Laura is coming, so prepare :
The chaste Ristormel can alone
Replace the loss of Avignon.

TO ROSE.

If by my death I win a tear,
O Rose, why should I linger here ?
If my departure cost you two,
Alas ! I shall be loth to go.

* By Simone Memmi, on the inner cover of a missal. [Note by Landor.]

The portrait is still in the possession of Lady Graves-Sawle, to whom Landor sent it. 'Simone Memmi,' Landor tells us elsewhere, 'the first of the moderns who gave roundness and beauty to the female face, neglected not the graceful air of Laura. Frequently did he repeat her modest features in the principal figure of his sacred compositions, and Petrarcha was alternately tortured and consoled by the possession of her portrait from the hand of Memmi.'—Works, 1876, viii., 432.

The verses 'To Rose,' that follow, were also sent to Miss Paynter, now Lady Graves-Sawle.

LOVE'S SECRETS.

Poplar ! I will not write upon thy rind
   Ianthe's cherisht name,
Which it would grieve me should another
    find,
   And the same station claim.

Ours, O Ianthe, ours must never meet,
   Tho' here we tarry long.
To hear the whisper of the leaves is sweet,
   And that bird's even-song.

One sweeter I have bidden thee to check
   In fear of passer by,
Who might have seen an arm about a
    neck ;
   So timorous am I.

IANTHE'S NAME.*

' Cannot you make my name of Jane
Sound pleasanter ? Now try again,'
Said she. At once I thought about
The matter, and at last cut out

* Mr. Sidney Colvin has quoted some unpublished verses of Landor's on the invention of the
names, Ione and Ianthe. The 'smart ring'd robber'

A letter from Greek alphabet,
And had it, as I thought, well set;
'Twas then 'Ianthe.' Soon there came
A smart ring'd robber with a claim,
You find it in his wardrobe stil,
More he would have, but never will.

CALLED PROUD.

If I am proud, you surely know,
Ianthe! who has made me so,
And only should condemn the pride
That can arise from aught beside.

was Lord Byron; and the phrase suggests an explanation of the lines:

> 'Wearers of rings and chains!
> Pray do not take the pains
> To set me right.'

Curious that Landor makes no reference to Ovid's 'Ianthe.' In an unpublished fragment he says: 'A name was converted by the magic of a Greek letter (θ) from a monosyllable into a trisyllable; and the fresh Ianthe was seized by the pet poet of the day, and offered by him to a Deity in the clouds. No hue and cry was raised after it. Trespassers have carried off weightier materials from my higher quarries: it were uncharitable to close the gate against a gleaner, and indecorous to snatch a cock's feather from his hat-band.'

THE LOVER.*

Now thou art gone, tho' not gone far,
It seems that there are worlds between us ;
Shine here again, thou wandering star !
Earth's planet ! and return with Venus.

At times thou broughtest me thy light
When restless sleep had gone away;
At other times more blessed night
Stole over, and prolonged thy stay.

A DREAMER'S TALE.

Dreamer I ever was by night and day.
Strange was the dream that on an upland bank
My horse and I were station'd, and I saw
By a late gleam of an October sun
The windows of a house wherein abode
One whom I loved, and who loved me no less—
And was she not drawn back ? and came not forth
Two manly forms which would impede her steps ?
I was too distant for them to discern
My features, but they doubted : she retired ;

* This is Landor's heading to the lines, which
may refer to the separation we read of in the
beautiful poem, beginning :

   ' Ianthe ! you are called to cross the sea,
     A path forbidden me.'

Was it into her chamber? did she weep?
I did not at that hour, but in the next
Silently flowed tear after tear profuse.
There are sweet flowers that only blow at night,
And sweet tears are there bursting then alone.*
    I turn'd the bridle back and rode away,
Nor saw her more until a loosen'd bond
Led her to find me a less happy man
Than she had left me, little happy then,
For hope had gone with her and not return'd.
She lookt into my eyes, fixt upon hers,
And said 'You are not cheerful, tho' you say
How glad you are to see me here again.
Is there a grievance? I have heard there is,
And the false heart slips down and breaks the
        true;
I come to catch it first; give it me back;
Sweet fruit is no less sweet for being bruiz'd.'
    Thus at brief intervals she spake and sigh'd;
I sigh'd, too, but spake not: she then pursued,
'Tell me, could it be you who came so far
Over the sea to catch a glance at one
You could not have?   Rash creature! to incur

* These two lines, slightly altered, were printed
by themselves in 'Heroic Idyls,' p. 228. The lady
of the poet's dream was doubtless Ianthe.

Such danger! was it you?   I often walkt
Lonely and sad along that upland bank,
Until the dew fell heavy on my shawl,
And calls had reacht me more and more distinct,
Ah me! calls how less willingly obey'd
Than some I well remember not so loud.'

INCONSISTENCY.*

Spring smiles in Nature's face with fresh delight,
　With early flowers her mother's brow adorn-
　　ing;
When morning comes, I wish again for night,
　And when night comes, I wish again for
　　morning.

TO IANTHE IN ADVANCING AGE.

The violets of thine eyes are faded,
　[Surviving] ill their radiant noon,
Nor will thy steps move on unaided
　By friendly arm, alas! how soon.

Well I remember whose it was
　They sought; no help they wanted then;
Methinks I see the maidens pass
　In envy, and in worse the men.

* Verses something like these may be found in
' Last Fruit,' p. 394, with the date, Brighton, 1807.

TO IANTHE GROWING OLD.

For me you wish you could retain
The charms of youth ; the wish is vain,
Ianthe !   Let it now suffice
To pick our way with weaker eyes :
They cannot light it as of yore
Where Pleasure's sparkling fount ran o'er.
Time spares not Beauty, Love he spares,
Who covers with his wing grey hairs.

IANTHE'S DAUGHTER.*

To thee, Maria, now within thy tomb,
God seem'd to promise many years to come.
A gift beyond the rest to Him we owe,
He left one image of thee here below.

TO LUISINA.†

Sweet as it is to hear a voice
    Dense crowds and distant lands above,
Yet in Luisina's I rejoice
    More deeply, voice of truth and love.

* Madame de Pereira Sodre.   See Landor's verses on this lady's marriage, Works, 1876, viii., p. 49.

† Miss de Pereira Sodre was Ianthe's granddaughter.

To me was it bequeath'd by one
  Who little thought her nursling child,
When she from earthly friends had gone
  In distant climes and deserts wild,

Columbia's youth should melt or cheer,
  With plaintive and with sportive song,
Or that her groves his name should bear
  Who loved so fondly and so long.

ON THE HEIGHTS.

The cattle in the common field
  Toss their flat heads in vain,
And snort and stamp ; weak creatures yield
  And turn back home again.

My mansion stands beyond it, high
  Above where rushes grow ;
Its hedge of laurel dares defy
  The heavy-hooft below.

THE PHILOSOPHER.

He who sits thoughtful in a twilight grot
Sees what in sunshine other men see not.

I walk away from what they run to see,
I know the world, but the world knows not
   me.

ADVICE TO A POET.

If you are jealous as pug-dog, O poet,
Button your bosom tight, and never show it.
If you are angry at the world's disdain,
What the world gives you, give the world again.
The Muses take delight in poets' sighs,
But they hear few ascending from the wise.
' *The more the merrier* ' (wicked jades !) they say,
Laugh in your face, and turn their own away.

TOLERANCE.

  Mobs I abhor, yet bear a crowd
  Which speaks its mind, if not too loud.
  Willingly would I hear again
  The honest words of pelted Payne.*
  Few dared such homely truths to tell,
  Or wrote our English half so well.

  * Thomas Paine, author of the ' Rights of Man,'
for whom Landor professed to have a certain liking.
See Works, 1876, vi., 157.   De Quincey said that
Aroar, in ' Gebir,' was too Tom Paineish.

INVITATION.

If there be any who would rather
Short thyme from steep Hymettus gather,
Than thro' Hyrcanian forests trudge
In heavy boots, knee-deep in sludge,
Come, here is room enough for you,
There will be round about but few.

THE POET WHO SLEEPS.

One day, when I was young, I read
About a poet, long since dead,*
Who fell asleep, as poets do
In writing—and make others too.
But herein lies the story's gist,
How a gay queen came up and kist
The sleeper.

    ' Capital !' thought I.
' A like good fortune let me try.'

* Clement Marot, Landor says in a note, but he was forgetting his history. It was Alain Chartier, the most ill-favoured man in France, whom Margaret Stuart, wife of the Dauphin, kissed on his mouth, ' de laquelle sont issus tant d'excellent propos, matières graves et paroles élégantes.' In prose Landor has told the story correctly. See Works, 1876, iii., 39.

Many the things we poets feign.
I feign'd to sleep, but tried in vain.
I tost and turn'd from side to side,
With open mouth and nostrils wide.
At last there came a pretty maid,
And gazed; then to myself I said,
'Now for it!'   She, instead of kiss,
Cried, 'What a lazy lout is this!'

THE POET WIDE AWAKE.*

Kisses in former times I've seen
Which, I confess it, rais'd my spleen:
They were contrived by Love to mock
The battledore and shuttlecock.
Given, return'd: how strange a play
Where neither loses all the day,
And both are, e'en when night sets in,
Again as ready to begin!
I am not sure I have not plaid
This very game with some fair maid.
Perhaps it was a dream; but this
I *know* was not: I *know* a kiss
Was given me in the sight of more
Than ever saw me kist before.

* Written July 8, 1860.

Modest as winged angels are,
And no less brave, and no less fair,
She came across, nor greatly fear'd
The horrid brake of wintery beard.

POET AND BUTTERFLY.

A poet sate in bower; there soon came nigh
With flappings up and down a butterfly.
Her name was Gloriosa; 'twas a name
Given at her birth by one who bore the same.
He saw its likeness, and he loved its ways
And gaudy colours in all sunny days.
' Ah !' sigh'd the poet, ' soon such days are over,
And our best plumage books and bindings cover.
Vainly we flutter, vainly are we loth
To leave our heritage to grub and moth.

WIDCOMBE CHURCHYARD.*

Widcombe ! few seek in thee their resting-place,
Yet I, when I have run my weary race,
  Will throw my bones upon thy churchyard
    turf;

* Mr. Forster, in his ' Life of Landor,' gives the
first stanza.   Landor purchased a plot of ground in
the churchyard at Widcombe, near Bath, where he
hoped to be buried.

Although malignant waves on foren shore
Have stranded me, and I shall lift no more
  My hoary head above the hissing surf.
Perhaps my dreams may not be over yet,
And what I could not in long life forget
  May float around that image once too dear;
Perhaps some gentle maiden passing by,
May heave from true-love heart a generous sigh,
  And say, ' Be happier, thou reposing here.'

CERVANTES.*

Cervantes was among my first delights,
Nor was forgotten in maturer age;
I dare not ask myself if Freedom urged
My steps to Spain more powerfully than he,

* Landor's memory played him a strange trick when he wrote these verses. He never saw the birthplace of Cervantes, who, moreover, was born in Alcara de Henares, in New Castile. While serving in Spain as a volunteer in 1808, Landor's journeys were confined to the northern province. Most of his three months in the country he spent in the neighbourhood of Aguilar — 'impenetrable, marble-turreted,' and ' in Reynosa's dry and thrift-less dale.' He would have liked to see Madrid, he

When that inveterate and infuriate foe
Of England and of Europe vaulted o'er
The Pyrenees.   I went there not unarm'd,
Nor left unhonour'd, tho' my stay was brief.
When Blake retreated to unsafe Seville
I stayed behind, but would not go aboard,
Tho' Digby call'd to welcome me, but went
To view La Mancha, where no human step
Disturb'd the silence, where the lizard clung
Upright and panted on the sultry wall.
My sword was idle, not the hand that bore it.
There were who wanted that, nor sued in vain.

---

told Southey, but feared lest a battle might be
fought in his absence.   It follows that he had no
opportunity of visiting either La Mancha or New
Castile.   In an Imaginary Conversation, however,
between Don Ferdinand and Don John Mary Luis,
first printed in 1829, mention is made of a foolish,
heretic Englishman who, on a hot day in August,
when 'the very lizards panted for breath, and
hardly clung against the walls,' visited Santillana,
'the birthplace of one Gil Blas' (Works, 1876, vi.,
318).   Landor was a great admirer of Le Sage.
'Show me,' he wrote, 'any style in any language
so easy, so diversified.'   But for 'the glorious wit,
Cervantes, who shattered the last helmet of knight
errantry,' his regard passed admiration.

O birthplace of Cervantes! proud of *him!*
Proud of the giver of another world!
Proud of immortal poets! hast thou risen
Only to fall again?   Bring back the hour
(Ah, couldst thou!) when I rode along thy
      downs
While war raged under me; some duty done,
I slept more soundly where the cistus helpt
My slumber, and the weaker thyme gave way.

DANIEL DEFOE.

Few will acknowledge all they owe
To persecuted, brave Defoe.
Achilles, in Homeric song,
May, or he may not, live so long
As Crusoe; few their strength had tried
Without so staunch and safe a guide.
What boy is there who never laid
Under his pillow, half afraid,
That precious volume, lest the morrow
For unlearnt lesson might bring sorrow?
But nobler lessons he has taught
Wide-awake scholars who fear'd naught:
A Rodney and a Nelson may
Without him not have won the day.

DANIEL DEFOE.

Strangers in vain enquire, for none can show
Where rests thy mutilated frame, Defoe !
Small men find room enough within St. Paul's,
The larger limb'd must rest outside the walls.
Be thou content, no name hath spred so
    wide
As thine, undamaged stil by time and tide.
Never hath early valour been imprest
On gallant Briton's highly-heaving breast
So deeply as by Crusoe ; therefor Fame
O'er every sea shall waft your social name.

JEFFREY CRITICISING SOUTHEY.*

Jeffrey ! the rod and line lay by,
Or only fish for little fry.
On dace and gudgeon you may fare,
Too deep for you lies Derwent Char.

* Landor heartily disliked the *Edinburgh Review* and its editor. 'I was once asked,' he wrote to Southey, ' whether I would be introduced to this gentleman. My reply was : " No, nor to any other rascal." I like to speak plainly, and particularly so when the person of whom I speak may profit by it.'

WILLIAM GIFFORD.*

Hold hard! let puffing Giff reach first
The sacred spring, for fierce his thirst.
Press not too nigh lest he bespatter
Each rival with the muddied water.

WITS AND BORES.†

There are few wits who never speak ill
In prose or rhyme, such wits are Jekyl
And Luttrell : like this couple let us
Gather our honey from Thymettus :

* Landor liked Gifford of the *Quarterly* even less than he liked Jeffrey. The animosity was reciprocal, and Gifford saw in Landor 'a most rancorous and malicious heart:'—'Memoirs of John Murray,' i. 164.

† Writing to Southey in August, 1832, Landor told a story of a breakfast-party, at which he himself and Jekyl were present. It was at Dr. Parr's, and Sir James Mackintosh was also among the guests. Mackintosh — very inaccurate, Landor notes, not only in Greek but in Latin—said something about the *Anabásis*. 'Very right, Jemmy,' was the Doctor's comment, '*Anabásis* with you, but *Anábasis* with me and Walter Landor.' The anecdote is not altogether pertinent ; but I cannot recall any other mention of Mr. Jekyl in Landor's writings. Henry Luttrell wrote 'Advice to Julia.'

Let the kid suck, the mother graze,
Nor pelt the poor old buck that strays.
Those thirst the most who are as dry as
Gifford or bell-weather Mathias.
At flabby pens why frown offended?
By the best blade can they be mended.

MEN OF THE DAY.

Disparage not our age, such thought were
    wrong,
Ask not a poet is it worth a song;
To this ye might hear Tennyson reply
At times in accents deep, at times in high.
Here has been in our iland one great man
Who, beyond all, the race of glory ran.
Beneath the rising and the setting sun,
The helm and scymeter of Wellesley shone.
And who was he* who later [dared] to
    brave
The icy barrier of the Baltic wave?
Nor have our gentle poets since been mute,
Although contented with their softer flute.
O'er the wide Continent, despotic Power
Is seen in threatening thunder-clouds to lour,

* Admiral Sir Charles Napier.

And there if any loftier heads remain
They raise them not, aware 'twould be in vain.
From thousand *city bards* no voice is heard
Above the twitterings of a household bird.
While in our happy Britain there is stil
Breath left the trumpet of fair fame to fill.

JAMES I. OF SCOTLAND.

Have I no sympathy for kings ?   I have,
And plant a laurel on a royal grave.
James !   I will never call thy fortunes hard,
A happy lover and unrival'd bard.
For Chaucer, Britain's first born, was no more,
And the Muse panted after heavy Gower.

DESPOTS OF EUROPE.

Regain, ye despots, if ye can your thrones,
And drown with trumpeting a nation's groans.
For you in vain do watchful dragons keep
The lonely darksome intervals of sleep.
Ere long shall justice from high heaven descend,
And man's worst grief, when you she smites,
    shall end.

POLAND AND THE CZAR.*

Who would not throw up life to be exempt
From Europe's execration and contempt,
From all the written and unwritten scorn
Of thousands round, and thousands yet unborn,
That withers with a tongue of quenchless
    shame
Wilhelm and Nicholas and one more name?

THE RISING IN POLAND.

March, tyrant, o'er Sarmatia's blooded plain.
One hand may do what armies dare in vain.
Few of thy race have died a natural death,
Or drawn without fierce pangs their latest
    breath.
What have I spoken? inconsiderate word!
Natural their death is, by the drug or sword,
Who burn the cottage and the babe within,
No doubt to purge him of original sin.

* 'I am confident you would not willingly omit the verses I wrote last night, after reading the atrocious threat of the Czar, ordering the death-stroke to be given to Poland within ten days. . . . The shock given me by the Czar has made my head, after whirling round, come nearly right again.'—Landor to A. de Noé Walker.

Some call it cruel, others think it odd
In those who govern by the Grace of God:
Others impatiently rush forth with arms
Across the wastes which lately were their farms;
Sickle and scythe are all that now remain,
But these shall reap their harvest—not of grain.

WILLIAM I. OF PRUSSIA.

William! great men have sat upon the throne
Beneath whose weight thy Prussian subjects
    groan.
Frederic and Frederic's father bravely fought,
And did, tho' scepter'd, some things as they
    ought.
Illiterate was the latter, and severe
To those about him, more so to those near.
The wittiest and the wisest of their times
Bestow'd on him what he could spare of
    rhymes,
And in his closet saw no sin or shame
(For who was there to do it or to blame?)
In washing what he call'd his *dirty linen*,
Which, like us others, he was apt to sin in.
Thy smear'd and daily change wants cleansing
    more
Than what those bloody ones required before.

TO AMERICA, ON ITALY.

My eyes first saw the light upon the day*
It dawn'd on thee, but shone not brightly yet,
America! and the first shout I heard
Of a mad crowd, around a madder king,
Was shout for glorious victory, for blood
Of brethren shed by brethren.

        Few the years
Before I threw my cricket bat along
The beaten turf to catch the song of France
For freedom—ah poor slave! free one short
  hour.
Glorious her women: will she ever bear
A man, whom God shall raise so near Himself
As Roland, Corday, and the Maid of Arc,
Deliverer of her country, vanquisher
Of her most valiant chiefs, enraged to see
The captive lilies droop above the Seine?

 America! proud as thou well mayst be
Both of thy deeds and thy progenitors,
Thy hero, Washington, stands not alone;
Cromwell was his precursor, he led forth

* Landor was born on January 30, 1775. His
earliest book of poetry contains an Ode to George
Washington.

Our sires from bondage, Truth's evangelist,
And trod down, right and left, two hostile
 creeds.
Brothers of thine are we, America!
Now comes a sister, too long held apart.
Lo! Italy hath snapt her double chain,
And Garibaldi sounds from shore to shore.

SICILY.

Again her brow Sicania rears
Above the tomb : two thousand years
Have smitten sore her beauteous breast,
And War forbidden her to rest.
Yet War at last becomes her friend
And shouts aloud, ' Thy grief shall end,
Throw off the pall, and rise again,
A homeless hero breaks thy chain.'

ORSINI'S LAST THOUGHTS.*

Condemn'd I die, by one who once conspired
With me, and stood behind me while I struck.
Where are the Gracchi, where are those twin-
 stars

* It was on January 14, 1858, that Felix Orsini
attempted to assassinate the Emperor and Empress
of the French by means of explosive bombs. Two

Who guided men thro' tempests? are they
   set
Never to rise again?   No, there remain
For Italy, brave guides to lead her sons
In the right path, altho' its end be death.

I would live one day longer, only one,
Not that a wife and children might embrace

---

years earlier he had been Landor's guest at Bath,
having come with letters of introduction from Italian
gentlemen living in London.   'Miserable Orsini !'
Landor wrote to Mr. Forster, on the day after the
outrage; 'he sat with me two years ago at the
table on which I am now writing.   Dreadful work !
horrible crime !   To inflict death on a hundred for
the sin of one !   Such a blow can serve only to
awaken Tyranny, reverberating on the brass helmets
of her Satellites.'   In the excitement of the time,
says Mr. Forster, Landor was publicly named as
friendly to Orsini's later opinions; and was at some
pains to declare, as publicly, that the imputation
was grossly unjust.   Landor was also acquainted
with Allsop, in whose name Orsini's passport was
made out, and who was accused of complicity in
the plot against the Emperor.   He had met
him at Charles Lamb's.   Landor's belief in the
righteousness of tyrannicide was not without limita-
tions.

A neck so soon to let its weight fall off,
The eyes yet rolling round, nor seeing them ;
For the worst stroke comes from that word
    adieu,
And heavier than the stroke is the recoil.

Rome's ravens feed not the deserted child,
But God will feed it, and in God I trust :
His breath shall cleanse the temple long pro-
    faned,
And the caged doves within the portico
Flutter, leap up, and wildly flit around
Hearing the scourge of him who lets them
    out.

Free thou wast never long, beloved Rome !
But free thou wast, and shalt again be free.

NICE, THE BIRTHPLACE OF GARIBALDI.*

In fields of blood however brave,
Base is the man who sells his slave ;
But basest of the base is he
Who sells the faithful and the free.
Nicæa ! thou wast rear'd of those
Who left Phocæa crusht by foes,

* Written on June 13, 1860.

14—2

And swore they never would return
Until the red-hot ploughshare burn
Upon the waves whereon 'twas thrown:
Such were thy sires, such thine alone.
Cyrus had fail'd with myriad host
To chain them down; long tempest-tost,
War-worn and unsubdued, they found
No refuge on Hellenic ground.
All fear'd the despot: far from home
The Cimri saw the exiles come,
Victorious o'er the Punic fleet,
Seeking not conquest but retreat,
A portion of a steril shore
Soliciting, nor vantage more.
There rose Massilia.   Years had past
And once again the Tyrian mast
Display'd its banner, and once more
Phocæans won it; on thy shore,
Landed their captives and raised high
Thy city named from victory.
Firmly thou stoodest; not by Rome,
Conqueror of Carthage, overcome.
Fearing not war, but loving peace,
Thou sawest thy just wealth increase.
Alas!   What art thou at this hour?
Bound victim of perfidious Power.

Bystanders we (oh shame !) have been
And this foul traffic tamely seen.
  Thou wast not heart-broken yet,
Nor thy past glories will forget ;
No, no, that city is not lost
Which one heroic soul can boast.
So glorious none thy annals show
As he whom God's own voice bade go
And raise an empire, where the best
And bravest of mankind may rest.
Enna for them shall bloom again
And peace hail Garibaldi's reign.

SPAIN.

Lately 'twas shown that usurpation
Will suit no more the Spanish nation.
The luckless king of Mountain Mill*
In his campaign succeeded ill.
Sadly we fear the holy oil
In these hot days will waste and spoil ;
Let those who vend it get fresh grease
To smear him, chanting ' *Rest in Peace.* '

* The Count of Montemolin, who renounced his
claim to the Spanish throne in April, 1860.

IRELAND.

Ireland! now restless these eight hundred years!
Thy harp sounds only discords; day and night
Thy cries are cries for murder, friend or foe
It matters not.   Ah! when wilt thou repose?
When will thy teachers cease to preach against
All human laws? when bid obey thy prince,
Nor listen to another who assumes
To rule as God's vicegerent, yet who knows
That God is truth and God's command is peace?
'*Ye can not serve two masters*,' so said He,
Yet thou rejectest one who rules thy land,
Obeying one who calls across the sea,
Who claims the tribute and who girds the
    sword.

MILO AND PIO NONO.

Milo of Croton with a stroke
    Of his clencht fist could fell an ox;
But when he tried to split an oak,
    He found himself ' in the wrong box.'

He thrust both hands into the slit.
    It closed on them; he stampt and swore.
Would it not open?   Not a bit;
    It only held him fast the more.

Pio could bring down kings and princes
   By dozens, but there comes at last
An ugly customer who winces
   And kicks amain, and holds him fast.

O, Mother Church! what hast thou done?
   I hardly think thy fornications
Deserve the curse of such a son;
   A plague to thee, a scourge to nations.

Ah! but thou taughtest him to lie
   When first he sat upon thy knee;
Now thy weak frown he dares deny,
   And spits upon thy rotten see.

CHURCHMEN.

Churchmen there are who, after one more
    bottle,
Would even leave old port to kick the shin
Of dissident, but would not push aside
The last half-cup of luke-warm tea to loose
A martyr from the stake. And some there are
Who curb and spur, and make curvet and
    prance
That piebald steed the jockies call *Religion.*
By Jove! what quarters has the jade! what
    thews!

GRACE.

There was a clergyman who used to say
(Morn, noon, and night) his prayers every day ;
Perhaps they all do ; but this worthy priest
Long before dinner-time outran the rest.
Now mark the sequel of his earnest words,
After the solemn reading of the Lord's,
' O Lord ! be merciful to me a sinner !
Sally ! what is there in the house for dinner ?'

RELIGION IN DANGER.*

Alas ! infidelity darkens the land,
Which we must enlighten with faggot and
    brand,
For how can we ever expect any good
From churchmen who question if hares chew
    the cud ?

* ' This I wrote on seeing in the *Times* last
Tuesday the persecution of Bishop Colenso.
Landor to A. de Noé Walker—MS. correspon-
dence [? March, 1863].

ARTHUR DE NOÉ WALKER.

Arthur, who snatches from the flames
Scraps which Oblivion vainly claims,
And givest honest Newby those
Which rhyme holds separate from prose,
Add to the flyleaf or fag-end
These few last scratches of a friend.

ON THE GRAVE OF GARROW AT FLORENCE.*

How often have we spent the day
In pleasant converse at Torquay;
Now genial, hospitable Garrow,
Thy door is closed, thy house is narrow.
No view from it of sunny lea
Or vocal grove or silent sea.

AZEGLIO.†

Azeglio is departed : what is left
To Italy, of such a son bereft ?
Hope, valour, virtue, all the Arts—they rest,
Tho' sadly sighing, on a mother's breast.

* The father of Theodosia Garrow, afterwards
Mrs. T. A. Trollope.

† Massimo Taparelli, Marchese di Azeglio, after
distinguishing himself as painter, author, patriot,

ON MY SISTER.*

Of many I have mourn'd the death,
But thou the most, Elizabeth!
Of all our house the first thou wast
Who would thy Walter have embraced;
Therefor I will not dry the tears
The daily thought of thee endears.

SIR CHARLES NAPIER.

How could you think to conquer Scinde,
And leave no enemy behind?
Indus rolls onward fifty streams,
But none so noisome as the Thames.

EPITAPH FOR GENERAL W. NAPIER.

Last of the Giants! thou whose vigorous
    breast
Bore many wounds, and sank by none opprest,

---

and statesman, became Prime Minister to the King
of Sardinia.   The lines seem to refer to his journey
to England. He outlived Landor, who dedicated
to him his 'Last Fruits off an old Tree.'

   * Elizabeth Savage Landor, his eldest sister,
died February 24, 1854, aged seventy-seven years.

Earth covers thee, like all, and War and Peace
Upon thy tomb from equal discord cease.
Heard was the trumpet that was blown from
    Scinde,
And the true brother would not halt behind.

A CHILD TO A BIRD.

Bad little bird ! why art thou gone,
    Deserter of my breast ?
Why to the wood ?   In wood is none
    So soft and safe a nest.

Good little birds fly not from home,
    Nor, when we call 'em, linger.
I will not scold thee, only come
    And perch upon my finger.

I long to feel thy claw, I long
    To hold thy beak in mine,
Then loosen it.   Come, bring thy song,
    No song so sweet as thine.

CHILD AGAIN.

Question.

And what became of that old man
    Whose name I could not spell,
So fond of that sad boy who ran
    Pelting the birds ?   Come, tell.

Answer.

My pretty child ! the tale all through
    I would have gladly told
When I repeated all I knew
    About both young and old.

Question.

But surely you will let me hear
    What, when Œnone died,
Became of those two faithful deer,
    And how they must have cried ?

Answer.

They wept, I doubt not, but they left
    The shed, their haunt before,
Of her who fondled 'em bereft,
    And fed them at the door.

Question.

I am (and are not you ?) afraid
    The dogs who came from Troy
Would presently find where they stray'd,
    Cheer'd on by wicked boy.

Answer.

No hound (or hunter crueler
    Than hound) would hurt those two,
Who lay upon the grave of her
    Whose love had been so true.

TO A MASTIF.

Mastif! why bark at me who love thy race?
To fear thee I should deem it foul disgrace.
In thy dominions I have walked alone,
Nor ever bore a stick or rais'd a stone.
Against the little, low, and wiry-hair'd,
I must confess it, I would go prepared:
To the high-crested creature, dog or man,
I do whatever services I can,
But to caress or compliment a cur
Of either species, stiffly I demurr.

TO MY DOG.

Giallo!* I shall not see thee dead
Nor raise a stone above thy head,
For I shall go some years before,
And thou wilt leap up me no more,
Nor bark, as now, to make one mind
Asking me am I deaf or blind.
No, Giallo! but I must be soon,
And thou wilt scratch my grave and moan.

* 'Poor Giallo died yesterday. Poor dog! I miss his tender faithfulness.' Contessa Baldelli to her brother, November 30, 1872.

TO A TREE.

Acacia, how short-lived is all thy race!
Slender was I, but thou wast slenderer,
When I began to notice thee; thy stem
Hath long been wrinkled, long before my brow.
Well I remember tossing up against
Thy lowest tassel my blue-ribbon'd hat,
And how it hung there till the rake was call'd
To rescue it, nor that light work refused.
Well I remember the limp hat, and aim
To bring the blossom down within my reach,
And break it—boys too soon are mischiefous
Almost as men—and how the blossom caught
And held to it what would have caught the
    blossom.
Thus happens it sometimes with weightier
    things.

Acacia! low thou liest, and the axe
Hath scattered wide thy weak and wither'd
    limbs,
But I will treasure up one particle
Before some strangers take thy wonted place,
Small, delicate, requiring nurse's aid;
Pamper'd and rear'd for parlour company
They soon will be, thou not so soon, forgotten.

EPIGRAMS.

Epigrams must be curt, nor seem
Tail-pieces to a poet's dream.
If they should anywhere be found
Serious, or musical in sound
Turn into prose the two worst pages
And you will rank among the sages.

TO AN OLD POET.

' Turn on the anvil twice or thrice
Your verse,' was Horace's advice :
Religiously you follow that,
And hammer it til cold and flat.

THE GOOD-NATURED FRIEND.

Some if they're forced to tell the truth
Tell it you with a sad, wry mouth,
And make it plainly understood
Such never was their natural food.

FUGITIVE PIECES.

Fugitive pieces ! no indeed,
How can those be whose feet are lead ?

THE SONNETTEER.

Sonnet is easy in the Tuscan tongue,
And poets drop it as they walk along.
A young professor was invited once
To try his hand, and this was the response :
' I never turn'd a sonnet in my life,
I had no mistress, and I *have* a wife.
If anything should happen, then the Muse
To help me at a pinch might not refuse.
Fancy and tenderness, I have enough
For that occasion—but she is *so* tough.'

IDLE WORDS.

They say that every idle word
Is numbered by the Omniscient Lord.
O Parliament ! 'tis well that He
Endureth for Eternity,
And that a thousand Angels wait
To write them at thy inner gate.

ON THESE EPIGRAMS.

Germans there are who sweat to cram
Conundrum into epigram ;
And metaphysics overload
A cart that creaks on sandy road.

All who look out for quaint and queer
Are sadly disappointed here:
Our only aim has been to fit
A ready rhyme to ready wit.

WILLIAM VON SCHLEGEL.

Schlegel; where first I met thee was at Bonn:
I knew thee but by name, and little thought
The only mortal who could comprehend
Shakespeare, in all his vastness, stood before
    me.
I wondered, when I lookt on thee, at tags
Of ribbon, buckles, crosses, round thy breast;
As, on their birthday, boys display new drums,
High feather in the hat and fierce cockade.
Is this the man, thought I, but held my tongue,
Who knew the heart of Shakespeare, and his
    ways
Thro' every walk of life, o'er land and sea,
And into regions where nor sea nor land
Are peopled, but where other Beings dwell,
Above, below.
        Schlegel, he recognized
In thee his privy-counselor, bade step

With him thro' treacherous courts, courts dark
    with blood,
Bade thee bare witness how Othello stabb'd
His Desdemona, bade thee hold the pall
Of virgin white that cover'd Juliet's bier,
Then gather daisies, rosemary and rue,
And columbine, as crazed Ophelia will'd.
No sadness ever toucht my heart like hers:
I think, but dare not own it, I have cried
As child, who to his tongue applies a bee
And, as he tastes the honey, feels the sting.
Master of mind, in every form it takes,
And universal as the Universe,
Is Shakespeare, ambient as the air we breathe,
Bright as the sun that warms it, vast and high
As that dispenser to all worlds around
Of light and life, wherever life exists:
Many are the stars that gem the throne of
    Night
But veil their lustrous eyes when he walks forth.
So are there poets in our hemisphere
Who glimmer, not obscurely; they approach,
Gazing with bated breath and front abashed:
Barr'd in a tower where none can touch them
    lie
His sceptre, sword and coronation robes.

MEMORIAL OF E. M. ARNDT.*

Arndt ! in thy orchard we shall meet no more
To talk of freedom and of peace revived.
We stood, and looking down across the Rhine
Heard fights and choral voices far below.
'What an enthusiastic song, O Arndt !' said I,
'Is that !' then smiled he, and he turn'd aside
My question.
   'Why not deem our Teuton tongue
Worthy to have been learnt with ancient
 Rome's
Which we converse in ? When an Attila,
Far less ferocious, far more provident,

* Toward the end of 1832, after a visit to England, where he had met Charles Lamb and Coleridge, Landor, on his way back to Fiesole, spent a few days at Bonn. There he saw William von Schlegel and Arndt. Of the former he wrote to Crabb Robinson : ' He resembles a little pot-bellied pony tricked out with stars, buckles, and ribbons, looking askance from his ring and halter in the market for an apple from one, a morsel of bread from another, a fig of ginger from a third, and a pat from everybody.' His interview with Arndt the next day, he said, ' settled the bile this coxcomb of the bazaar had excited.' One poem to Arndt was published in ' Last Fruits,' p. 475.

Than his successor, storm'd the Capitol,
He broke no oaths, no vows, no promises;
But he who since laid waste our fertile fields,
And handcuft our weak princes, broke them all.
I am among the many better men
Whose head he had devoted: I am he,
The framer of that anthem; they who now
Sing it would then have sung it o'er my grave,
And found their own in singing it.'
He stopt
Suddenly, then ran forward; swiftly ran
The septuagint, and overtook the youth
Who carried the light weight of ten years less,
For he had seen an apple drop and roll
Along the grass: he stoopt and took it up
And wiped the dew away, and gave it me.
'Keep it, for there are better in the house,'
Said he, ' and this is over-ripe; one pip
Keep in remembrance of our converse here.'
I sow'd them all; but kill'd were the new-born
Ere slender stem could rear its first twin-leaves,
And all were swept away maliciously
By one who never heeded sage or sire.

———

A PASTORAL.*

Damon was sitting in the grove
With Phyllis, and protesting love;
And she was listening; but no word
Of all he loudly swore she heard.
How! was she deaf then? no, not she,
Phyllis was quite the contrary.
Tapping his elbow, she said, 'Hush!
O what a darling of a thrush!
I think he never sang so well
As now, below us, in the dell.'

TO LESBIA.

I loved you once, while you loved me;
  Altho' you flirted now and then,
It only was with two or three,
  But now you more than flirt with ten.

* Mr. Kenyon told the story, in a somewhat different form, to the late Mrs. Andrew Crosse. Landor, on his honeymoon, was entertaining his bride with a reading of his own poems. Suddenly she rose, with the exclamation: 'Oh, do stop, Walter! There's that dear, delightful Punch performing in the street. I *must* look out of the window.'

TO LESBIA.

I swore I would forget you; but this oath
  Brought back your image closer to my breast:
That oaths have little worth your broken troth
  Had taught me; teach my heart like yours to
    rest.

SAPPHO TO PHAON.

Time has not made these eyes so dim;
  I never have complain'd of *him*:
Of one how different I complain!
  Come, Phaon, bring them light again.

A WARNING TO KINGS.*

My mule! own brother of those eight
Which carried Ferdinand in state;
Alas! how many a dublado
I paid for thee to Infantado.
None but his Excellence and Grace
Possesses thy unequal'd race.
I grieve not that my gold is gone,
  My noble Mule! I grieve alone

* A reminiscence of Landor's campaigning days
in Spain.

That thou, the highest of the high
And whitest of the white, shouldst die
Under the plate some robber steals
Stabb'd by another at his heels.
Thou never stumbledst; but my humble
Prayer is that thou some day wilt stumble,
And break the neck of him whose reign
Is now extending over Spain.

INFLUENCES.

There are two rivals for the heart of Man,
Pleasure and Power; first comes into the field
Power, while yet Pleasure has not learnt to
    smile
At the fond teacher bending o'er the task.
Years fly fast over him, then Pleasure calls
Nor waits, but shows before him various paths,
All verdant, fresh, and flowery: midst of these
He wearies and he stretches out his arms
To some fair object beckoning from beyond.
Even at the feast of Love he sits morose
If any should sit opposite this one
And hold sly converse with prone ear too close
To ear as prone.
            Tell me, ye whom the Muse
Hath wean'd from Pleasure, tell me have not ye

Been also jealous, tho' afar from Love,
Afar from Beauty, and in dell or bower
Immerst; and have not oft your temples
    throb'd,
Withering the moss whereon they would repose
When Power was leading, high above your
    heads,
A happier brother onward.
                              We are all
Babes at some moment of our after-life.

ADVICE IN RETURN FOR CANTOS.

Ah! heap not canto upon canto
Which you must drag a weary man to,
But try such themes as may be brief
And, if they tire, soon comes relief.
The Greeks have done it, and our neigh-
    bours
The French succeed in these light labours.
Firm mansions oft are built of stone
Less than a waggon-load each one;
And oaks that o'er the forest frown
For pleasure-boats are not cut down.
A poem of ten thousand verses
Is parent of as many curses.

PISA.*

At Pisa let me take my walk
Alone, where stately camels stalk,
And let me hope to catch the eye
Of pheasant on the ilex by,
That he alight and find the bread
Crumbled for him, and none instead.
Robins in earlier morn may come
And make my winter house their home.

AT ARNO'S SIDE.

Pisa ! I love thee well, altho'
Compell'd by friendship now I go
Where golden cones of pine illume
No more with fragrant warmth my room,
Nor patient camels crouch, or stand
Awaiting from a well-known hand
To crunch with palm-long teeth the tips
Of stubborn thorn thro' hardy lips,
Then stalk along with stately stride
To rest again at Arno's side.

* Where Landor lived, 1820-21. ' We gave a
dinner yesterday in the forest of Pisa. . . .   What
adds considerably to the Oriental aspect of the
scene are the droves of camels wandering through
it.'   (Lady Blessington.)

But camels! winter will return
When cones from your old pines shall burn,
Changeless in form: I wish that we
The same throughout our lives could be,
With warmth as temperate waste away
And cheerful to the last as they.
Some lower necks, good mothers, bring
For me to pat ere pass the Spring.

TO THE RIVER AVON.

Avon! why runnest thou away so fast?
Rest thee before that Chancel where repose
The bones of him whose spirit moves the
    world.
I have beheld thy birthplace, I have seen
Thy tiny ripples where they played amid
The golden cups and ever-waving blades.
I have seen mighty rivers, I have seen
Padus, recovered from his fiery wound,
And Tiber, prouder than them all to bear
Upon his tawny bosom men who crusht
The world they trod on, heeding not the cries
Of culprit kings and nations many-tongued.
What are to me these rivers, once adorn'd
With crowns they would not wear but swept
    away?

Worthier art thou of worship, and I bend
My knees upon thy bank, and call thy
    name,
And hear, or think I hear, thy voice reply.

LAST WORDS.

Pretty Anne Boleyn made a joke
On her thin neck, just when the stroke
That was to sever it was nigh,
And show'd how innocence should die.
The wittier and the wiser More
With equal pace had gone before.
Earlier in Athens died the sage
Who's death o'er Plato's puzzling page
Sheds its best light: well matcht with
    these
Was shrewd and sturdy Socrates.
He laught not at the gods aloud,
For that would irritate the crowd;
But, not to die in debt, he said,
To the few friends about his bed,
'Let Æsculapius have his fee
For radically curing me.
A gamecock he deserves at least
So catch and take one to his priest.'

FOND AND FOOLISH.

If ever there was man who loved
And wept for it, that man has proved
Our earlier authors are less wrong
Than we are in our native tongue ;
That *fond* and foolish, tho' in name
Unlike, are in effect the same.

THE PHOCÆANS.*

O'erpast was warfare : youths and maidens
    came
From the Ligurian shore, and the Tyrrhene
And the far Latian, to console the brave
After their toils, and celebrate the rites
Of the same gods.   Hymen stood up aloft ;
His torch was brighter than the deadly glare
Lately so reverenced by a crouching throng
In Druid worship, over blacken'd oak
Leafless and branchless : hymns were sung
    before
That smiling youth whose marble brow was
    crown'd

* These lines, Landor says in a note, would have
closed ' The Phocæans.'   See above, p. 135.

With summer flowers, and Love's with earlier
    spring's.
Apollo stood above them both, august,
Nor bent his bow in anger more than Love.
Here was no Python; worse than Python one
Had vext the land before his light came down.
Here stood three maidens, who seem'd ministers
To nine more stately, standing somewhat higher
Than these demure ones of the downcast smile:
Silent they seem'd; not silent all the nine.
One sang aloud, one was absorb'd in grief
Apparently for youths who lately bled;
Others there were who, standing more elate,
Their eyes upturn'd, their nostrils wide ex-
    panded,
Their lips archt largely; and to raise the hymn
Were lifted lyres; so seemed it; but the skill
Of art Hellenic forged the grand deceit.
Night closed around them, and the stars went
    down
Advising their departure: when they went
I too had gone, for without them I felt
I should be sad, when from above there came
A voice—it must have been a voice of theirs,
It was so musical—and said ' Arise,
Loiterer, and sing what thou alone hast heard.'

' Inspire me then,' said I, 'O thou who standest
With the twelve maidens round !
                              Was it a dream ?
I thought the Delian left his pedestal
A living God, I thought he toucht my brow ;
Then issued forth this hymn, the very hymn
I caught from the full choir, the last they sang,
' Incline a willing ear, O thou supreme
Above all Gods ! Jove liberator ! Jove
Avenger ! to Phocæa's sons impart
The gift of freedom all our days, and peace
To hold it sacred and with blood unstain'd.
And do thou, consort of the Omnipotent !
Bestow thy blessing on our rescued few,
And grant the race, adoring thee, increase.'

GREECE.

A voice descending from the Parthenon
Cried ' Rise up, sons of Hellas !'   It was borne
Beyond the land of Pelops, and beyond
The Ægæan and Ionian sea, across
The Adriatic, to that wounded man
Who gave a kingdom and who lost a home.
They whom he saved dared strike him.   Death
      dared not,
Standing above his head with lifted dart.

The voice assuaged his anguish; on his lips
Ye might have fancied hung these warning
    words :
' My friends, my future comrades ! stand com-
    pact,
And drive the intruder from your sacred soil.
Be vigilant ; look westward ; he who feign'd
Deliverance is enslaver ; he attunes
His fiddle to the steps of dancing slaves,
And stamps on toes that keep not to his time.
  The Briton has been free two hundred years,
Longer the Hollander, Helvetia's son
Preceded him, and won the upland race ;
Be Hellas fourth, no sluggard in the field.
Their glory none of those had merited
Had they forbidden God to hear the prayers
Of his weak children in their mother tongue.
The human body rises not at once,
But member after member ; its extremes
Are first to stir, and they support the rest.
  Give freedom if thou wouldst thyself be free,
Resurgent Hellas ! force not on the neck
Of others that spiked yoke thou hast thrown
    off ;
Leave his one God to the quell'd Osmanli,
Nor tread the papal slipper down at heel,

Nor drive the quiet Martin from thy gate.
Take and hold stedfastly one more advice.
Remain within thy ancient boundary.
Worst of all curses is the thirst of rule
O'er wide dominion : where is Babylon ?
Where Carthage ? Earth's proud giant brood,
      they lie
Along the dust ; the dust alone remains
Imperishable and by age unchanged.
Marble and bronze may crowd the peopled
      street,
Men will ask who were those ? I place my palm
On a small volume which contains his words
Who rous'd and shook and would have saved
      thy land,
Demosthenes, the patriot who disdain'd
To live if life must be a despot's gift.
Cherish his memory, teach thy sons his lore.'

APOLOGY FOR THE HELLENICS.

None had yet tried to make men speak
In English as they would in Greek.
In Italy one chief alone
Made all the Hellenic realms his own ;
He was Alfieri, proud to teach
In equally harmonious speech.

Soon, wondering Romans heard again
Brutus, who had been dumb, speak plain.
Corneille stept forth, and taught to dance
The wigs and furbelows of France.
In long-drawn sighs the soft Racine
Bestrewed with perfumed flowers the scene.
I wish *our* bard, our sole dramatic,
Had never overlookt the attic:
Tho' dried the narrow rill whereby
The bards of Athens loved to lie,
Yet Avon's broader deeper stream
Might have brought down some distant dream,
Nor left for trembling hand like mine
To point out forms and feats divine.
Children, when they are tired with play,
Make little figures out of clay,
And many a mother then hath smiled
At the rare genius of her child;
But neither child nor man will reach
The godlike power of giving speech.
Fantastic forms weak brains invent . . .
Show me Achilles in his tent,
And Hector drag'd round Troy, show *me*
Where stood and wail'd Andromache;
Her tears through ages still flow on,
Still rages, Peleus, thy stern son.

HYMN TO PROSERPINE.

Look up, thou consort of a king whose realm
Is wider than our earth, and peopled more,
A king, a god; look up, Persephone!
Behold again the land where thou wast born,
The field where first thy mother from her
    knee
Let down, with both her hands, thy dimpled
    feet,
Cautiously, slowly, where the moss was soft
And crowds of violets bow'd their heads around.
From thy calm region cast thine eyes again
On Enna, where sang once thy virgin choir,
And gather'd flowers for thy untroubled brow;
Here never wilt thou shudder at a car
Of ebony and iron, nor bite his arm
Who lifted thee above the sable steeds,
Snorting and rearing, and then rushing down,
Nor hearing the shrill shrieks of those behind.
Happy art thou, and happy all thou seest
Around thee, far as stretch the Elysian plains,
Where weapons bright as in the blaze of war
Are interchanged by chiefs who strove at Troy,
And music warbles round the concave orb
Of golden cup, well-drain'd, of roseate wine.

But, O Persephone! what wasting herd
O'erruns the meadow of thy joyous youth!
What monsters lurk amid those chestnut groves,
And ilexes, and trample down the bank
Of rivers where thou freshenedst thy limbs
Glowing with brightness thro' the boughs
    above!
Dwarf Cyclopses, more hateful than the huge,
Crunch daily in their cavern brave men's bones,
And howl against the pilot who directs
The sad survivers thro' the swelling sea.
    The largest hearts are overladen most,
They swell to bursting; wrath dries up the tear
Of grief; strong men sink at the feet of weak!
Dastards, where once rose heroes, and where
    rang
The hymn of triumph sang by bards as bold,
Depopulated thy cities and thy fields,
Follow'd by slaves in arms.
                   Persephone!
Thou art persuasive; none but thou alone
Can bend the monark; raise thy cheek against
His rigid beard and kiss his awful brow;
Promise him, swear to him by Styx itself,
That thou wilt give him twice the worth of
    what

He once made drop from thee he well knows
    where;
Remind him how his true and constant love,
While other gods swerv'd wide from constancy,
Hath made him dearer than thy earlier friends,
And charm'd away even thy fond mother's grief;
Tell him that he, true king, must hate the false;
Tell him to let them pass the Styx unhurt,
And walk, unstay'd, unterrified, until
Phlegethon drown their cries in liquid fire.

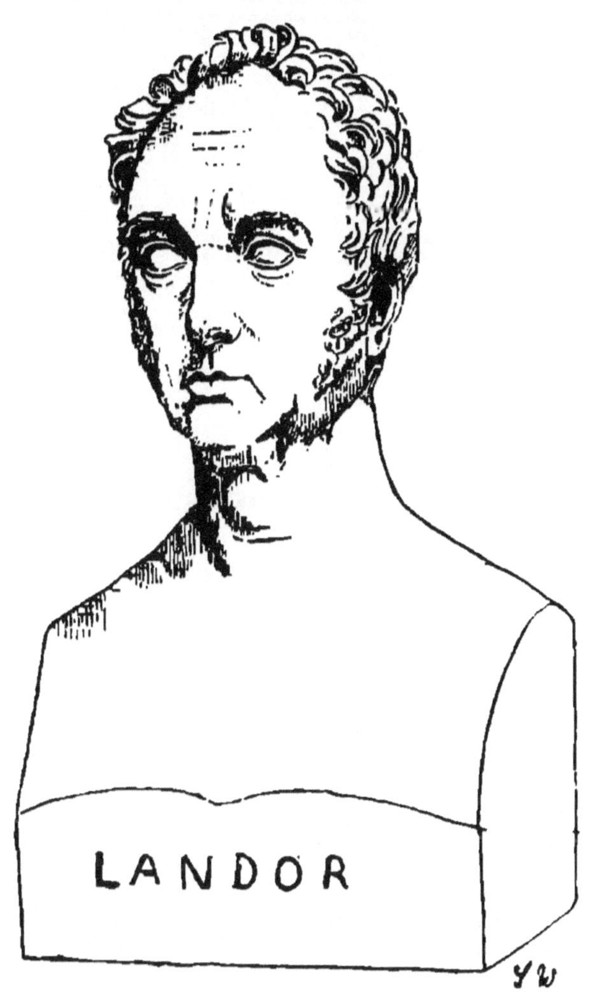

PORTRAIT OF WALTER SAVAGE LANDOR.

(From a Bust by Gibson.)

To face p. 244.

BIBLIOGRAPHY.

PART I.

1795.—The Poems of Walter Savage Landor. London: Cadell and Davies.

[Of the thirty-two poems contained in this volume, six are quoted, in part or at length, in Forster's 'Life of Landor.' The remainder have not been reprinted.]

1795.—A Moral Epistle; respectfully Dedicated to Earl Stanhope. London: Cadell and Davies.

[In verse. An attack upon William Pitt.]

1798.—Gebir; a Poem in Seven Books. London: Rivingtons.

1800.—Poems from the Arabic and Persian, with Notes, by the author of 'Gebir.'

Warwick: printed by H. Sharpe, High Street, and sold by Messrs. Rivingtons, St. Paul's Churchyard, London.

[Reprinted, but without some of the notes, in 'Dry Sticks.' See 1858.]

1800.—POETRY, by the Author of 'Gebir,' and a Postscript to that Poem, with Remarks on some Critics. Warwick: Sharpe, Printer.

[Landor's friend, Mr. Isaac Mocatta, persuaded him to suppress this volume (Forster's 'Life,' i. 140); but there are two copies of it, one imperfect, at South Kensington Museum. Some of the poetry was published in 1802 and afterwards; other pieces, of which Mr. Forster quotes a couple ('Life,' i. 191), were cancelled.]

1802.—POETRY, by the author of 'Gebir.' London : Rivingtons.

[This volume contained, 'The Story of Chrysaor'; two fragments of an epic, 'From the Phocæans,' and 'Part of Protis's Narrative'; and some English and Latin verses. 'The Story of Chrysaor' was reprinted by Mr. Forster ; the fragment 'From the Phocæans' by Mr. Crump. Of the shorter English poems all except one may be found in the 1876 edition of Landor's works.

The verses beginning ' Is haughty Spain again in
arms ?' were reprinted in ' Heroic Idyls,' but not
elsewhere.]

1803.—GEBIR; A POEM IN SEVEN BOOKS, by
Walter Savage Landor; second edition.
Oxford: Slatter and Munday.

1803.—GEBIRIUS; POEMA. SCRIPSIT SAVAGIUS
LANDOR. Oxford: Slatter and Munday.

[The Latin version of ' Gebir.']

1806.—SIMONIDEA. Bath: Meyler; and London:
Robinson.

[English and Latin verses. All but two of the
English poems and a portion of a third have been
reprinted.]

1809.—THREE LETTERS, WRITTEN IN SPAIN,
to D. Francisco Riguelme, command-
ing the 3rd Division of the Gallician
Army. Printed for G. Robinson and
J. Harding, London.

1810.—AD GUSTAVEM REGEM.

1812.—COUNT JULIAN: A TRAGEDY. London:
Murray.

1812.—COMMENTARY ON MEMOIRS OF MR. FOX. London : Murray.

[Mr. Sidney Colvin believes that there is only one copy in existence, in the possession of Lord Crewe.]

1813.—LETTERS to the *Courier*, signed Calvus.

[These were reprinted in the form of a pamphlet, with an additional letter, dated December 30, 1813. A copy of the pamphlet, with MS. corrections in Landor's hand, was among the papers in his desk.]

1815.—IDYLLIA NOVA QUINQUE HEROUM ATQUE HEROIDUM. Oxford.

1820.—IDYLLIA HEROICA DECEM. Partim jam primo partim iterum atque tertio edit Savagius Landor. Pisa.

1821.—POCHE OSSERVAZIONI, ETC., di Walter Savage Landor. Naples.

1824.—IMAGINARY CONVERSATIONS OF LITERARY MEN AND STATESMEN, by Walter Savage Landor, Esq. Vols. i. and ii. London : Taylor and Hessey.

[Vol. i. contains a dedication, dated Florence, October 1822, to the author's brother-in-law,

Major - General Stopford, Adjutant - General in the Army of Columbia; Vol. ii. is dedicated from Florence, November, 1823, to the Spanish General, Mina. Each volume contained eighteen conversations, all of which reappeared in the same or an altered shape in later editions.]

1826.—IMAGINARY CONVERSATIONS OF LITER-ARY MEN AND STATESMEN, etc. Vols. i. and ii. The second edition, corrected and enlarged. London: Colburn.

[The order of the conversations is not the same as in the first edition.]

1828.—IMAGINARY CONVERSATIONS OF LITER-ARY MEN AND STATESMEN, etc. Vol. iii. London: Colburn.

[Contains twenty new conversations. That between Ines de Castro, Don Pedro and Dona Blanca was afterwards turned into blank verse. The remaining conversations were all reprinted, with more or less alterations. The dedication, dated June 3, 1825, with postscript, July 1, 1827, is to ' Bolivar, the Liberator.']

1829.—IMAGINARY CONVERSATIONS, etc. Vols. iv. and v. London: Duncan. De-scribed in a separate title - page as

'Imaginary Conversations,' second
series, vols. i. and ii.

[Vol. iv. contained fifteen new conversations;
vol. v. twelve. The former was dedicated,
May 5, 1826, to General Sir Robert Wilson;
the latter, on August 18, 1826, to the Earl of
Guilford. In the preface Landor expresses his
sorrow at the death of Dr. Parr. The old dedi-
cations were omitted in later editions. 'Mina
gave orders,' Landor wrote, 'to kill a woman;
Bolivar was a coxcomb and imposter, having been
200 miles distant from the battle he pretended to
have won; and Wilson is worse than a Whig.']

1831.—GEBIR, COUNT JULIAN, AND OTHER
POEMS, by Walter Savage Landor,
Esq. London: Moxon. Dedication
to Francis George Hare, Florence,
January 1, 1827.

CONTENTS.

Gebir.	Ippolito di Este.
Count Julian, a tragedy.	Gunlaug.
Ines de Castro at Cintra.	Ianthe.
Ines de Castro at Coim-bra.	Miscellaneous Poems.
	On the Dead.

[Several of the poems had appeared in
'Simonidea.' All but thirteen are reprinted in
Works, 1846 and 1876.]

1834.—CITATION AND EXAMINATION OF WILLIAM
     SHAKESPEARE, etc.   To   which   is
     added a conference of Master Edmund
     Spenser, a Gentleman of Note, with
     the Earl of Essex, Touching the State
     of Ireland in 1596.   London: Saunders
     and Otley.
[Reprinted in Works, 1846 and 1876.]

1836.—DEATH OF CLYTEMNESTRA.   Friendly
     Contributions for the Benefit of Three
     Infant Schools in the Parish of Ken-
     sington.   Printed solely for the Right
     Honourable Lady Mary Fox.
[Reprinted in Works, 1846 and 1876.]

1836.—PERICLES AND ASPASIA, by Walter
     Savage Landor, Esq.   Two vols.
     London: Saunders and Otley.

[Vol. i. contains a dedication to the Earl of
Mulgrave, Lord - Lieutenant of Ireland, and
Advertisement, dated Villa Fiesolana, July 4,
1835.   Vol. ii. contains an Ode to General
Andrew Jackson, President of the United States,
dated July 3, 1835; and an appendix entitled
‘ Reflections on Athens at the decease of Pericles.’
For the Ode see Works, 1876, vol. viii., p. 134.
Mr. Forster did not reprint the ‘ Reflections.’

' Pericles and Aspasia ' was reprinted, with some alterations, in Works, 1846 and 1876.]

1836.—THE LETTERS OF A CONSERVATIVE ; in which are shown the only means of saving what is left to the English Church, addrest to Lord Melbourne. London : Saunders and Otley.

[Not reprinted.]

1836.—TERRY HOGAN ; an Eclogue lately discovered in the Library of the Propaganda at Rome, and now first Translated from the Irish. Thereunto is subjoined a dissertation by the Editor, Phelim Octavius Quarle, S. T. P. Γυναικες ωλεσαν με. — Euripides. London : printed by J. Westheimer and Co.

[Never reprinted, and not reprintable. The copy in the British Museum, the only one I have seen, was given to Dr. Garnett by the late Mrs. De Morgan in 1873.]

1837.—A SATIRE ON SATIRISTS, AND ADMONITION TO DETRACTORS. London : Saunders and Otley.

[Not reprinted.]

1837.—THE PENTAMERON AND PENTALOGIA.
    London : Saunders and Otley.

[1. The Pentameron, or interviews of Messer
Giovanni Boccaccio and Messer Fr. Petrarcha,
when said Messer Giovanni lay infirm at his
Viletta hard by Certaldo ; after which they saw
not each other on our side of Paradise ; shewing
how they discoursed upon that famous theologian,
Messer Dante Alighieri, and sundry other matters.
Edited by Pievano D. Grigi.
    [2. The Pentalogia, or five dramatic scenes :
        Essex and Bacon.
        Walter Tyrrel and William Rufus.
        The Parents of Luther.
        The Death of Clytemnestra.
        The Madness of Orestes.
    [Reprinted in Works, 1846 and 1876.]

1839.—ANDREA OF HUNGARY AND GIOVANNA
        OF NAPLES, by Walter Savage Landor.
        London : Richard Bentley.

    [Two dramas; reprinted in Works, 1846
and 1876.]

1841.—FRA RUPERT.   London : Saunders and
        Otley.

    [Reprinted in Works, 1846 and 1876.]

1846.—The Works of Walter Savage Landor. Two vols. London: Moxon.

1847. — Poemata et Inscriptiones novis auxit Savagius Landor. Londini: Impensis Edwardi Moxon.

1847.—The Hellenics of Walter Savage Landor, Enlarged and Completed. London: Moxon.

[There is a dedication to Pope Pius IX., in which Landor says, ' Cunning is not wisdom; prevarication is not policy; and—novel as the notion is, it is equally true—armies are not strength: Acre and Waterloo show it, and the flames of the Kremlin and the solitudes of Fontainebleau.]

1848.—Imaginary Conversation of King Carlo-Alberto and the Duchess Belgoioiso. London: Longmans.

[Reprinted in ' Last Fruit ' and in Works, 1876.]

The Italics of Walter Savage Landor. London: Reynell and Weight.

[This volume, now a rare one, contained seven short poems; all reprinted in ' Last Fruit,' and again in Works, 1876, vol. viii.]

1851.—POPERY; BRITISH AND FOREIGN, by Walter Savage Landor. London: Chapman and Hall.

[Reprinted in ' Last Fruit.']

1853.—THE LAST FRUIT OFF AN OLD TREE, by Walter Savage Landor. London: Moxon.

[The dedication, in Italian, to the Marchese di Azeglio. Reprinted, with some exceptions, in Works, 1876.]

1853.—IMAGINARY CONVERSATIONS OF GREEKS AND ROMANS, by Walter Savage Landor. London: Moxon.

[With a dedication to Charles Dickens, ' to register my judgment that, in breaking up and cultivating the unreclaimed wastes of Humanity, no labours have been so strenuous, so continuous, or half so successful, as yours.']

1854.—LETTERS OF AN AMERICAN, MAINLY ON RUSSIA AND REVOLUTION, edited by Walter Savage Landor. London: Chapman and Hall.

[Not reprinted.]

1856.—ANTONY AND OCTAVIUS; SCENES FOR THE STUDY, by Walter Savage Landor, London: Bradbury and Evans.

[These scenes are dedicated to Edward Cappern, 'poet and day-laborer at Bideford, Devon.' Reprinted in Works, 1876, vol. vii.]

1856.—A LETTER FROM W. S. LANDOR TO R. W. EMERSON. Bath: published by E. Williams.
[Not reprinted.]

1858.—DRY STICKS, FAGOTED BY WALTER SAVAGE LANDOR. Edinburgh: James Nichol. London: James Nisbet and Co.

[These dry sticks kindled to anything but love, and the law's wrath well-nigh consumed him who collected them. The volume is dedicated to ' L. Kossuth, President of Hungary.' Portions of the volume only were reprinted in Works, 1876.]

1859.—THE HELLENICS OF WALTER SAVAGE LANDOR, COMPRISING HEROIC IDYLS, etc. New edition, enlarged. Edinburgh: J. Nichol.

[The dedication is to General Sir W. Napier. Reprinted in Works, 1876.]

1862.—LETTERS OF A CANADIAN. [See above, p. 125.]

1863.—HEROIC IDYLS, WITH ADDITIONAL POEMS, by Walter Savage Landor. London: Newby.

[Dedication to the Hon. Edward Twisleton, Florence, August 25, 1863. Portions of this volume were reprinted in Works, 1876.]

1869.—WALTER SAVAGE LANDOR; A BIOGRAPHY, by John Forster. Two vols. London: Chapman and Hall.

[This is the edition of Forster's Life of Landor cited in the text.]

1876.—THE WORKS AND LIFE OF WALTER SAVAGE LANDOR. Eight vols. London: Chapman and Hall.
Vol. i. Biography, by John Forster.
Vol. ii. Classical Dialogues, and Citation and Examination of William Shakespeare.
Vol. iii. Conversations of Sovereigns and Statesmen. Five Dialogues of Boccaccio and Petrarcha.
Vol. iv. Dialogues of Literary Men.

Vol. v. Dialogues of Literary Men (continued); Dialogues of Famous Women ; Pericles and Aspasia ; Minor Prose pieces.

Vol. vi. Miscellaneous Conversations.

Vol. vii. Gebir ; Acts and Scenes and Hellenics.

Vol. viii. Miscellaneous poems, and Criticisms on Theocritus, Catullus, and Petrarcha.

REPRINTS, Etc.

1882.—SELECTIONS FROM THE WRITINGS of WALTER SAVAGE LANDOR, arranged and edited by Sidney Colvin. London : Macmillan.

1883.—IMAGINARY CONVERSATIONS, by Walter Savage Landor. Five volumes. London : Nimmo.

[A reprint of the prose Conversations in Works, 1876.]

1884.—ENGLISH MEN of LETTERS—LANDOR, by Sidney Colvin. London : Macmillan.

1886.—IMAGINARY CONVERSATIONS, by Walter Savage Landor. With introduction by Havelock Ellis. London : W. Scott.

[Contains thirty-three Conversations.]

1889.—THE PENTAMERON AND OTHER IMAGINARY CONVERSATIONS, by Walter Savage Landor. Edited by Havelock Ellis. London: W. Scott.

1890.—PERICLES AND ASPASIA, by Walter Savage Landor. Preface by Havelock Ellis. London: W. Scott.

1890.—PERICLES AND ASPASIA, by Walter Savage Landor. Edited by C. G. Crump. Two vols. London: Dent.

1891.—IMAGINARY CONVERSATIONS, by Walter Savage Landor. With bibliographical and critical notes by C. G. Crump. Six volumes. London: Dent.

1892.—POEMS, DIALOGUES IN VERSE, AND EPIGRAMS, by Walter Savage Landor. Edited, with notes, by C. G. Crump. Two vols. London: Dent.

[A selection.]

1892.—CITATION AND EXAMINATION of WILLIAM SHAKESPEARE, by Walter Savage Landor. London: Chatto and Windus.

1892.—THE LONGER PROSE WORKS OF WALTER SAVAGE LANDOR. Edited, with notes, by

C. G. Crump. Two vols. London:
Dent.

[Contains 'Citation and Examination of Shakespeare';
'Pericles and Aspasia,' 'Pentameron'; five Conversations
not in Works, 1876; and Critical Essays on Theocritus,
Catullus, and Petrarcha.]

1895.—WALTER SAVAGE LANDOR; a Biography, by
John Forster. London: Chapman and
Hall.

[A new edition of the Biography, as published in Works,
1876.]

PART II.

1823.—London Magazine, July. Imaginary Conversation: Southey and Porson.

1832.—Philological Museum. (Cambridge, edited by Julius Hare.)
Vol I., Poemata Latina.
[Signed ' W. S. L.']

Imaginary Conversation: Solon and Pisistratus.
[Reprinted in Works, 1846 and 1876.]

1833.—Athenæum, January. Ode to Southey.
[Reprinted in Works, 1846 and 1876.]

---

* This list of Landor's innumerable contributions to magazines, reviews, and newspapers has yet to be completed.

1833.—Philological Museum. Vol. II.,
Imaginary Conversation: P. Scipio
Emilianus, Polybius and Panætius.

[Reprinted in Works, 1846 and 1876.]

[? A note on Cleon and Admiral Vernon.
Signed 'W. S.']

1834.—Book of Beauty. Imaginary Conversations: Rhadamistus and Zeno-
bia; Philip II. and Dona Juana
Coelho.

[Reprinted in Works, 1846 and 1876.]

1834.—Leigh Hunt's London Journal,
December 3. Ode to Joseph Ablett.

[Reprinted in Works, 1846 and 1876.]

1835.—Book of Beauty. Imaginary Conversation: Steel and Addison.

[Reprinted in Works, 1846 and 1876.]

1835.—Leigh Hunt's London Journal,
June 13. Verses: 'To the Sister of
Charles Lamb.'
July 11. Letter on 'Language and
Orthography.'

1836.—Book of Beauty. 'The Parable of
Asabel.'

[Reprinted in 'Literary Hours' and in Works,
1876, v., 593.]

1837. —Book of Beauty.
Imaginary Conversation. Colonel
Walker and Hattaji.

[Reprinted in Works, 1846 and 1876.]

Verses: 'Farewell to Italy!'
[Works, 1876, viii., 80.]

1837.—The Monthly Repository (edited by
Leigh Hunt). 'High and Low Life
in Italy.'

[A series of letters; not reprinted.]

1837.—Literary Hours by various Friends,
printed by George Smith, Liverpool,
for Joseph Ablett. This volume
contained six Imaginary Conversations, and 'The Parable of Asabel,' all
reprinted from the *Book of Beauty* and
Philological Museum; the Conversation: 'Bishop Shipley and Benjamin
Franklin'; and the 'Death of Hofer'—

all in prose: and a number of occasional poems.

[Reprinted, with one or two exceptions, in Works, 1876.]

1837.—THE TRIBUTE (edited by Lord Northampton.

 1. Orestes and Electra. Last scene.
 2. Luther's Parents. Dialogue in verse.

[Reprinted in Works, 1876, vols. v., and vii.]

1838.—BOOK OF BEAUTY. 'The Dream of Petrarcha.'

[Reprinted in Works, 1876, v., 590.]

1839.—BOOK OF BEAUTY.

 1. Anne Boleyn and the Constable of the Tower.

[Reprinted, Works, 1876, vii.]

 2. Henry VIII. and Northumberland.

[Reprinted, Works, 1876, vol. vii.]

1840.—Book of Beauty. Imaginary Con-
        versation ; Galileo, Milton and
        Dominican.
[Reprinted in Works, 1846 and 1876.]

Verses to Miss Rose Paynter.
[Reprinted, Works, 1876, viii., 145.]

1841.—Book of Beauty. Verses:
        ‘Pleasures away, they please no
        more.’
[Reprinted, Works, 1876, v., 433.]

1841.—Keepsake. Verses: ‘Torbay.’
[Reprinted, Works, 1876, viii., 78.]

1842.—Book of Beauty. Verses: ‘To Zoe,’
        June, 1808.
[Reprinted, Works, 1876, viii., 45.]

1842.—Keepsake.   ‘A Skolion from the
        Greek.’
[Not reprinted.]

1842.—Foreign Quarterly Review, July:
        ‘The Poems of Catullus.’
[Reprinted in Works, 1876, vol. viii.]

October: 'The Poems of Theocritus.'

[Reprinted in Works, 1876, vol. viii.]

1842.—BLACKWOOD'S MAGAZINE, December.
Imaginary Conversation: Southey
and Porson.

[Reprinted in Works, 1846 and 1876.]

1843.—BOOK OF BEAUTY.
Imaginary Conversation: Vittoria
Colonna and Michel Angelo.

[Reprinted in Works, 1846 and 1876.]

1843.—KEEPSAKE.
A Story of Santander.

[Reprinted in Works, 1846 and 1876.]

1843.—BLACKWOOD'S MAGAZINE.
January. Imaginary Conversation:
Tasso and Cornelia.
February. Imaginary Conversation:
Oliver Cromwell and Sir O. Crom-
well.
March. Imaginary Conversation:
Sandt and Kotzebue.
Verses: 'To my Daughter.'

[All reprinted in Works, 1846 and 1876.]

1843.—FOREIGN QUARTERLY REVIEW.
July. Francesco Petrarcha.
[Reprinted in Works, 1876.]

1844.—BOOK OF BEAUTY.
Imaginary Conversation: Æsop and Rhodope.
A Vision.
Verses to Lady Charles Beauclerk.
[All reprinted in Works, 1846 and 1876.]

1844.—KEEPSAKE.
Verses: 'Malvern.'
[Reprinted in Works, 1846 and 1876.]

1845.—BOOK OF BEAUTY.
Imaginary Conversation: Æsop and Rhodope, ii.
[Reprinted in Works, 1846 and 1876.]

1845.—KEEPSAKE.
Verses: 'Take the last flowers your natal day.'
[Reprinted in Works, 1846 and 1876.]

1846.—BOOK OF BEAUTY.
Imaginary Conversation: 'Tancredi and Constantia.'
[Reprinted in Works, 1846 and 1876.]

1846.—KEEPSAKE.
   Verses: 'One year ago my path was
   green.'
[Reprinted in Works, 1846 and 1876.]

1847.—BOOK OF BEAUTY.   Italian verses:
   'Veglia di Partenza.'

1847.—KEEPSAKE.   'A Dream of Youth and
   Beauty.'
      [Not reprinted.]

   Italian verses: 'Mi vien, mi vien da
   píangere.'

1848.—KEEPSAKE.
   Verses: 'On leaving my Villa.'
   [Not reprinted.]

1848.—EXAMINER, March 25.   Imaginary Conversation: 'Thiers and Lamartine.'
[Reprinted, Works, 1876, vol. vi.]

1849.—EXAMINER.   Letters to the Editor:
   July 7. 'The Pope temporal and
   spiritual.'
   July 28. 'France, Italy and the
   Czar.'

August 11. 'Austrian Cruelties.'
September 8. 'The comfortable state
of Europe.'

[Not reprinted.]

1850.—LEIGH HUNT'S JOURNAL, December 7.
Verses :

1. 'Instead of idling half my hours.'

[Reprinted, Works, 1876, viii., 172.]

2. 'Again to Paris ? Few remain.'

[Not reprinted.]

3. 'Love flies with bow unstrung
when Time appears.'

[Reprinted, Works, 1876, viii., 166.]

1851.—KEEPSAKE.
Dramatic Scene : 'Beatrice Cenci
and Clement VIII.'

[Reprinted, Works, 1876, vii., 342.]

1851.—EXAMINER.
March 13. 'Sir Benjamin Hall and
the Bishop of St. David's.'

[Letter, not reprinted.]

June 21, June 28 and August 2. Imaginary Conversation : Nicholas and Nesselrode.

[Reprinted, Works, 1876, vi., 585.]

August 16. ' Naples and Rome.'

[Letter, not reprinted.]

August 20 and 23.   Imaginary Conversation : Antonelli and Gemeau.

[Reprinted, Works, 1876, vi., 616.]

September 27.   Verses : ' To Meschid the Liberator.'

[Reprinted, Works, 1876, viii., 248.]

October 11.   Verses : ' Hast thou forgotten, thou more vile.'

[Reprinted, Works, 1876, viii., 251.]

October 25.   Verses : ' To Beranger at Tours.'

[Reprinted, Works, 1876, viii., 249.]

Verses : ' Hymn to America.'

[Reprinted, ' Last Fruit,' 477.]

December 13. 'Tranquillity in Europe.'
[Letter.   Reprinted in 'Last Fruit,' 348.]

Verses: 'Made our God again, Pope Pius.'
[Reprinted, Works, 1876, viii., 253.]

December 20. 'Finality in Politics.'
[Letter, not reprinted.]

Verses: 'Save from Thee, most Holy Father.'
[Not reprinted.]

December 27.   Verses: 'City of men, rejoice.'
[Reprinted, ' Last Fruit,' 481.]

' Ten letters to Cardinal Wiseman,' reprinted in *Last Fruit,* were also first published in the *Examiner* this year.

1851.—LEIGH HUNT'S JOURNAL.
February 1.   Verses:
'To Luisina at Paris.'
[Not reprinted.]

Verses to a Lizard:
> 'You pant like one in love, my Ramorino.'

[Reprinted, Works, 1876, viii., 188.]

Verses:
> ' If you go on with ode so trashy
> Cupples will seize the crutch and thrash ye.'

[Not reprinted.]

February 15. Verses:
> ' So then, I feel not deeply ! if I did.'

[Reprinted, Works, 1876, viii., 233.]

March 1. Verses:
> ' Nay, thank me not again for those.'

[Reprinted, Works, 1876, viii., 175.]

March 22. Verses:
> ' Horace and Creech !'

[Reprinted, Works, 1876, viii., 190.]

1852.—ATHENÆUM.
January 10. Imaginary Conversation: Alcibiades and Xenophon.

[Reprinted, Works, 1876, ii., 122.]

1853.—EXAMINER.

February 19. Imaginary Conversation: Archbishop of Florence and Francesco Madiai.
[Reprinted, Works, 1876, vi., 631.]

June 11. Imaginary Conversation: Nicholas and Nesselrode.
[Reprinted in Mr. Crump's edition.]

1854.—EXAMINER.

February 11. Imaginary Conversation: Nicholas and Diogenes.
[Reprinted in Mr. Crump's edition.]

December 2. Imaginary Conversation: Pio Nono and Antonelli.
[Reprinted in Mr. Crump's edition.]

1855.—LIFE AND CORRESPONDENCE OF THE COUNTESS OF BLESSINGTON, by Madden, contains an unpublished Imaginary Conversation: ' Lord Mountjoy and Lord Edward Fitzgerald.'

1855.—THE ATLAS.

April 28. ' To the people of England.'
[Not reprinted.]

Verses : ' The Four Georges.'
[Not reprinted.]

May 19. ' Failure of Negotiations.'
[Not reprinted.]

May 23. ' House of Commons'
Morality.'
[Letter.   Not reprinted.]

June 9.   Verses : ' A most puissant
picture-scouring prince.'
[Reprinted in ' Dry Sticks,' p. 35.]

July 14. ' A Lesson from the Crystal
Palace.'
[Letter.   Not reprinted.]

September 22. ' The Fall of Sebas-
topol.'
[Letter, not reprinted.]

September 29. Verses : ' Why should
not A—— meet the Czar ?'
[Reprinted in ' Dry Sticks,' p. 50.]

' The Christian and the Mahomedan.'
[Letter : see above, p. 148.]

October 6. A long letter on the execution of Count Louis Batthyany.

[Not reprinted.]

October 13. Two letters;
1. 'Dishonest conduct of the War.'
2. 'Royal Marriages.'
[Not reprinted.]

1855.--EXAMINER.

April 17. Imaginary Conversation: Ovid and the Prince of the Getæ.
[Reprinted in Mr. Crump's edition.]

August 4. Verses:
'Under the Lindens.'
[Reprinted in Works, 1876, viii., 281.]

1855.—FRASER'S MAGAZINE, November. Imaginary Conversation: Asinius Pollio and Licinius Calvus.
[Reprinted, Works, 1876, ii., 433.]

1856.—FRASER'S MAGAZINE, April. Imaginary Conversations: Alfieri and Metastasio; Menander and Epicurus, ii.
[Both reprinted in Works, 1876.]

1861.—ATHENÆUM.

March 2. Letter on the Pope's Temporal Power, dated Florence, February 26.

[Not reprinted.]

March 9. Imaginary Conversation: Virgil and Horace.

[Reprinted in Works, 1876, ii., 428.]

April 20. Letter on 'Fashions in Spelling.'

[Not reprinted.]

May 18. Imaginary Conversation: Milton and Marvel.

[Reprinted in Works, 1876, v., 150.]

October 12. Imaginary Conversation: Machiavelli and Guicciardini.

[Reprinted in Works, 1876, v., 145.]

1862.—ATHENÆUM.

August 16. Imaginary Conversation: Milton and Marvel, ii.

[Reprinted in Works, 1876, v., 156.]

INDEX.

ABLETT (Joseph), 20, 21, 89
Ablett's ' Literary Hours,' 14, 21,
    263
Abdul Medjid (Sultan 1839-1861),
    151
Abertawy (River), 67 ; verses on,
    186
Æschylus, Coleridge on, 162
Ahmed el Jezzar, 133
Albany (Countess of), 41-44,
    105 n.
Alexander VI. (Pope), 30
Alfieri (Victor), 19, 41, 105 ; death
    of, 44 ; and the Countess of
    Albany, an imaginary conver-
    sation, 41-43
Alvanley (Lord), 104
America, Landor and, 10, 128 ;
    verses to, 208, 270
' Andrea of Hungary ' (by W. S.
    Landor), 99, 253
' Anthony and Octavius : Scenes
    for the Study ' (by W. S. Lan-
    dor), 118, 256
Apology for the Hellenics, verses,
    240
Armenian question, the, 149, 150
Arndt (Ernest Maurice), verses
    to, 227
' Atlas,' Landor's contributions to
    the, 146, 273-275
Austin (Alfred), his ' Savonarola,
    a Tragedy,' 26, 36
Avon, verses to the river, 234

Aylmer (Bishop), 65
Aylmer (the Hon. Rose), 16,
    64-74, 186 ; a lock of her hair,
    74 ; tomb at Calcutta, 73
Azeglio (Marchese di), 217, 255

Baldelli (Contessa Geltrude), 5 ;
    Letters from, 6, 122, 221 n.
Bath, Landor at, 89, 108, 115,
    146, 147, 210 n.
Bembo (Cardinal), epigram on
    Venice, 125
Béranger (Jean de), 100, 270
Bewick (William), portraits of
    Landor by, 17, 19
Blackstone (Sir William), 56
Blackwood's Magazine and Lan-
    dor, 157, 158 ; Landor's con-
    tributions to, 266
Blessington (Countess of), 89
    103, 273 ; her account of W. S.
    Landor, 20 ; death and epitaph
    on, 113, 114
Boccaccio, 33, 93, 99, 100, 253
Boileau (Nicolas), 101
Bolivar (Simon), 10, 249, 250
Bonaparte (Napoleon), 137, 142-
    144
Bonn, Landor at, 227 n.
' Book of Beauty,' 66, 94, 262-268
Borgia (Lucretia), lock of hair,
    74
Bossuet (James de, Bishop of
    Meaux), 101

Bowles (Caroline, Mrs. Southey), 97
Boxall (Sir William, R.A.), portraits of Landor, 17, 23, 24
Boyle (Miss Mary), 23, 83, 92
Brougham (Lord), 102, 103, 108
Brown (Charles Armitage), 96
Browne (Professor E. G.), 133
Browne (Sir Thomas), 'Religio Medici,' 81
Browning (Mrs.), 119, 131, 134, 173
Browning (Robert), 78, 119; Landor on, 179, 180
Brownings, the, 119
Bulwer (Sir Henry Lytton-Bulwer, afterwards Lord Dalling), 15
Bulwer (Sir Edward Lytton), 101. See Lytton
Burke (Edmund), 143
Burns (Robert), 168, 173
Byron (Lord), 63, 109, 189; 'The Island,' 166; 'Don Juan,' 166; 'A Vision of Judgment,' 165; Landor and, 165-170; Landor on Byron's death, 167

Caldwell (Miss), 104, 105
Calvus,' 'Letters of, 140-145, 248
Campbell (Thomas), 62
Canova (Anthony), monument to Dante, 44
Cappern (Edward), 118, 256
Carlyle (Thomas), 41
Castlereagh (Viscount), 141
Cedar-tree, verses on, 4, 5
Cedar-wood, scent of, 2
Century Magazine, 23
Cervantes, verses on, 199
Chambers (Sir Robert and Lady), 72
Chantilly, 103
Chantrey (Sir Francis), 19
Chartier (Alain), 196
Chateaubriand, 101
Chatham (Lord), 141
Chaucer, spelling of, 123

Chesterfield (Lord), 104
'Chrysaor,' by W. S. Landor, 75, 134, 246
Clifton, Landor at, 78
Colenso (Bishop), 216 n.
Coleridge (Samuel Taylor) and Landor, 161-163; 'Lay Sermons,' 163
Coleridge, Lord, 164
Colvin (Mr. Sidney), 12, 24, 66, 83, 134, 248, 258
Combe (Lord Mayor), 57
Commons, House of, 52, 224
'Count Julian : a Tragedy,' by W. S. Landor, 247; Charles Lamb on, 175; Wordsworth on, 156
Courier, Letters to the, 137, 140, 248
Cousin (Victor), 100, 106
Cowper (William), 63, 125
Crimean War, Landor on, 148, 274, 275; Dr. Walker in, 116
Crosse (Mrs. Andrew), 229 n.
Crump (C. G.), editor of Landor's Works, 12, 13, 24, 135, 259
Czartoryski (Princess), 106

Dance (Nathaniel), portrait of Landor, 18
Dante, 33, 39; 'Divina Comedia,' 34, 44; monument at Florence, 44; tomb at Ravenna, 39
Dashwood (Mrs.), 14
Defoe (Daniel), 56; descendants of, 117; verses on, 201, 202
De Molandé, Countess. See Ianthe
De Quincey (Thomas), 54, 195 n.
De Tocqueville (Alexis), 100
Diana of Poictiers, 51
Dickens (Charles), 108, 181, 255
Don Quixote, Landor on, 176
D'Orleans, (Ferdinand, Duc), death of, 107
D'Orsay (Count Alfred), 104, 107, 113; portraits of Landor by, 21
D'Orsay (Lady Harriet), 98

'Dry Sticks,' by W. S. Landor, 66 n., 130, 256

Dumas (Alexandre), 52

Duncan (James, publisher), 127, 249

Edgeworth (Maria), 101

Eliot (George), ' Romola,' 26

Emerson (Ralph Waldo), 10, 114; Landor's letter to, 256

Evelyn (John), quoted, 4

Examiner, Landor's contributions to the, 103, 113, 146, 148, 273, 275

Fabre (M.), 42, 43

Field (Mr.), of Boston, publisher, 9, 11, 29, 41

Fiesole, Landor's villa at, 5, 88, 101, 114

Fisher (William), portraits of Landor by, 17, 22; portrait of Miss Rose Paynter, 94

Fitzgerald (Edward), 132; on Landor, 153

Fitzgerald (Mr. J. E., C.M.G.), 108, 109

Florentines, 35

Forester (Major the Hon. Charles), 104

Forster (Mr. John), 17; meeting with Ianthe, 89; his editions of Landor's Works, 12, 51, 82, 254, 257; Life of Landor by, 18, 23, 137, 245, 246, 257, 260

France, 34, 241; and Russia, 146

Francis I. (King of France), 51

French Revolution, the, 135; Alfieri on, 41

Garibaldi (Guiseppe), 29, 121, 209; verses on his birthplace, 211

Garrow (Mr. Joseph), verses on, 217

'Gebir,' by W. S. Landor, 67, 75, 134, 135, 153, 154, 245-247; Byron on, 166; Charles Lamb and, 175-177; de Quincey on, 195 n.; Sir Walter Scott and, 159; the sea-shell in, 159; Shelley and, 173; Wordsworth on, 156

Gell (Sir William), 105

Germany. poets of, 125, 224

Gherardesca Villa, 114. See Fiesole

Giallo (Landor's dog), verses to, 221; his death, *ib*.

Giannone (Pietro), 99; ' History of Naples ' by, 99 n.

Gibson (John, R.A.), bust of Landor by, 19, 20

Gifford (William), verses on, 203

'Gil Blas,' 200 n.

Giovanna di Napoli, 99, 100, 253

Goldsmith (Oliver), 125; his style, 56, 101

Gore House, Kensington, 22, 108, 114

Grammont (Duchesse de), 97

Grammonts, the, 113

Graves - Sawle (Lady), 23, 66, 111 n.; letters to, 111-113; portrait of, 66, 94; verses to, 187

Graves-Sawle (Sir Charles, Bart.), 94, 111 n.

Gray (Thomas), 125; ' Elegy in a Country Churchyard,' 53

Greece, verses on, 238

Guiccioli (Countess), 106

Guiche (Duc de), 107, 108

Hallam (Henry), 56

Hare (Archdeacon Julius), 261

Hare (Francis), 95, 98

Hayward (Mr. Abraham), 105

Hellenics, the, 85, 254, 256; Apology for (verses), 240

Hemans (Mrs. Felicia), 62

Henry IV. (King of France), 51

Henry of Luxemburg (Emperor), 33

Herbert (George), 53

Heroic Idyls, 70, 72, 82, 90, 116, 128, 129, 186, 191, 257; manuscript of, 9, 11

Holland (Sir N. D.). See Dance
Homer, 110 ; S. T. Coleridge on,
    162 ; his 'Iliad,' 62, 160 ; his
    'Odyssey,' 131
Hood (Thomas), 'The Song of
    the Shirt,' 124, 125
Hooker (Richard), 56
Houghton (Richard, Lord), 18.
    See Milnes.
Hunt (Leigh), meeting with Lan-
    dor, 74 ; 'London Journal,'
    179, 262 ; 'Monthly Reposi-
    tory,' 263 ; 'Journal,' 269
Hymn to Proserpine (verses),
    242

Ianthe, 70, 75-90 ; death of, 89 ;
    miniature of, 75-77 ; her name,
    188, 189 ; verses to, 188, 190-
    193
Ione, 75, 81 ; verses to, 185
Ipsley Court, Warwickshire, 1,
    3, 15
Ireland, verses on, 214
Italians, the issimi nation, 53

Jackson (Andrew), 251
James I. of Scotland, verses on,
    205
James (G. P. R.), 96
Jeffrey (Francis, Lord), verses on,
    202
Jekyl (Mr.), 203
'Joan of Arc and her Judge,'
    dramatic scene, 45-51
Johnson (Doctor), 72 ; his style, 56
Jones (Sir William), 131
Jonson (Ben), on spelling, 123

Keats (John), 125 ; 'Hyperion,'
    134 ; Landor and, 170-173 ;
    verses on, 171
Keepsake, Landor's contributions
    to the, 265-269
Kenyon (Mr. John), 23, 97, 229 n.
Kosciosko, 148
Kossuth (Louis), 16, 256 ; in
    England, 147 ; and the Turks,
    151

Lamartine (Alphonse de), 100, 268
Lamb (Charles) and Landor, 174-
    179 ; verses on, 178
Landor (Arnold), 116 n.
Landor (Rev. Charles), 112, 113
Landor (Miss Elizabeth), 1, 19
    letter to, 171 ; verses on, 218
Landor (Miss Ellen), 87
Landor (Rev. Robert), 19, 53 ;
    on Parr and de Quincey, 55
Landor (Walter Savage), Alfieri
    and, 41 ; on America, 9, 128 ;
    Lady Blessington on, 20 ; at
    Bonn, 227 ; Browning on, 78 ;
    on his contemporaries, 152-183 ;
    Garibaldi and, 29 ; visit to the
    Lambs, 178 ; on literary ex-
    humations, 7 ; portraits of, 17-
    24 ; on repetitions, 52 ; Spanish
    campaign, 199, 230 ; on him-
    self, 138
Landor (Walter Savage), Biblio-
    graphy, 245-276
Landor's Letters, to Contessa G.
    Baldelli, 5 ; to R. Browning,
    134, 137 ; to R. W. Emerson
    157, 256 ; to Mr. Field, of
    Boston, 30 ; to Mr. Forster, 23,
    100, 105, 162, 173, 210 ; to Lady
    Graves-Sawle, 96-113 ; to Kos-
    suth, 147 ; to Mrs. Paynter,
    69, 95 ; to Crabb Robinson,
    177 ; to R. Southey, 82, 131,
    138, 156, 171, 203 ; to A. de
    N. Walker, 7, 11, 17, 116-129,
    206, 216
Landor (Mrs. Elizabeth) on
    Byron, 168
Landor (Mrs. W. S.), 86 ; anec-
    dote of, 229 n.
Landseer (Sir Edwin), 108
'Last Fruit off an old Tree,' by
    W. S. Landor, 74, 91, 111, 192,
    218, 255
Laura, Petrarch's, 187
Ledru-Rollin, 106
Leipzig, battle of (1813), 137
Le Sage (Alain Réné), 200
Lesbia, verses to, 229, 230

'Letters of an American,' by W. S. Landor, 163, 255
'Letters of a Canadian,' by W. S. Landor, 125-127, 257
Linton (Mrs. Lynn), 127
'Literary Hours by Various Friends.' See Ablett
Liverpool (Lord), 140
Llantbony, 87, 137, 139 ; cedar-trees at, 4
Lorenzo (de Medici) the Magnificent, 36, 37
Lowell (James Russell), 10, 23
Luttrell (Henry), 203
Lyndhurst (Lord), 108
Lytton (Sir E. Bulwer-Lytton, Lord Lytton), 101, 124

Macaulay (Lord), 'Lays of Ancient Rome,' 63
Mackenzie (Miss, of Seaforth), 95
Mackenzie (Mr. Hector), 127
Mackintosh (Sir James), 57, 203 n.
Maclise (Sir D.), 108
Malakoff, the attack on the, 116
Marie Antoinette at Petit Trianon, 102
Marot (Clement), 196
Mary Stuart (Queen), 99
Massillon, 101
Mathias (Thomas James), author of 'Pursuits of Literature,' 96
Mazzolina da Ferrara, 124
Memmi (Simone), 187
Middleton (Dr. Conyers), 'Letters from Rome,' 123
Mignet (F. A.), 100
Milnes (R. Monckton, Lord Houghton), 56, 127
Milton's 'Paradise Lost,' 160; prose writings, 101 ; verification, 126
Mina (General), 249, 250
Mocatta (Mr. Isaac), 246
Molandè (Count de), 87. See Ianthe
Montemolin (Count of), 213

Moore (Thomas), 63 ; 'Life of Byron,' 170
Morgan (Lady), 101
Mulgrave (Earl of), 251

Napier (Admiral Sir Charles), 204 ; verses on, 218
Napier (Sir William), 104, 256 ; verses on, 218
Napoleon III. (Emperor), 103, 209
Nardi, monument to Alfieri by, 44
Newby (Mr. E.), 120, 125, 257
Nicholas I. (Czar of Russia), 206, 273
Norbury (Lord), 86

Omar Khayyam, 132
Orsini (Felix), 209, 210
Othman, an Arab poet, 133
Ovid, 'Metamorphoses,' 160 ; in praise of, 58-60 ; spelling of the name, 122

Paine (Thomas), 56, 195
Parr (Dr. Samuel), 54, 203 250 ; Landor on, 56
Paynter (Miss Rose), 265 ; Landor's letters to, 96-111. See Graves-Sawle (Lady)
Paynter (Mrs.), 68, 74, 93 ; Landor's letters to, 69, 95
Penni (Giov. Fr.), a picture by, 124
'Pericles and Aspasia,' by W. S. Landor, 104, 251, 259
Petrarcha, 33, 99, 253
Phoceans,' 'From the,' by W. S. Landor, 134, 135, 236, 246
Pico di Mirandola, 125
Pio Nono (Pope), verses on, 214, 254, 271
Pisa, Landor at, 172 ; camels at, 233 ; verses on, 233
Pius IX. (Pope), 254
Plato, 38
Poems from the Arabic and Persian, by W. S. Landor, 130-133, 245

' Poetry by the author of Gebir,' 134, 246

Poland and the Czar, verses, 206

Poland, Rising in, 206

Pomero (Landor's dog), 91 ; his death and epitaph, 92

Pope (Alexander), 78

Porson (Richard), 57, 157-159

Propertius, Landor misquotes, 164

' Protis's narrative,' 135, 136, 246

Quarterly Review, on ' Gebir,' 68 ; Landor and, 169, 203

Quillinan (Mr. Edward) and Landor, 158, 159

Raphael, 19

Récamier (Madame), 97, 106

Reeve (Miss Clara), 67

Richardson (Samuel), ' Clarissa Harlowe,' 61

Ristormel, 111-113, 187

Ritchie (Mrs. Richmond), 180

Robinson (H. Crabb), 23, 177

Rockingham (Marquis of), 143

Russell (Sir Henry), 16, 70, 71

Russia, Landor on, 146

Santillana, Landor at, 200

Sappho to Phaon, verses, 230

Savonarola, 26, 29 ; and the Prior of San Marco, Imaginary Conversation, 30-41

Schlegel (William von), verses to, 225, 227 n.

Scott (Sir Walter), 61, 63 ; compared to Froissart, 160 ; Landor and, 159-161 ; ' Marmion,' 160, 169 ; ' Waverley Novels,' 160, 161

Secundus (Johannes), 54

Sévigné (Madame de), 101

Shakespeare, 60, 109, 110, 121, 226, 251

Sheikh Dahir (Tahir), 132, 133

Shelley, 67, 125 ; Landor and, 172-174

Sicily, verses on, 209

Siena, Landor at, 120

Smith (Bobus), 57, 125

Smith (James), 43

Sodre (Madame de Pereira), 90, 193

Sodre (Miss Luisina de Pereira), 76, 90, 193 ; portrait of, 76, 91

Sorrento, 101

Southey (Robert), 22, 89, 98, 125, 134 ; ' Kehama,' 61, 62, 153 ; ' Triumphal Ode,' 137 ; ' Vision of Judgment,' 165 ; Byron and, 166 ; his second marriage 97 ; Landor and, 154, 155 ; on ' Gebir,' 67, 153, 154 ; on the ' Letters of Calvus,' 140 ; letter to Landor from, 139

Spain, Landor in, 139, 230 n. ; verses on, 213

Spenser (Edmund), ' Faery Queene,' 60

Stopford (General), 10, 249

Story (Miss Edith), verses to, 15

Story (Mr. William), 10, 119

Superlatives, absurd, 52

Swansea, Landor at, 67, 69

Swift (Dean), 77, 89 ; and Defoe, 56

Swift (Godwin), 77

Swift (Miss). See Ianthe

Swifte (Mr. Godwin), 79 ; death of, 86

Swifte (Mrs.). See Ianthe

Swinburne (Mr. Algernon), 183

Talleyrand, 106 ; ' Reminiscences,' 112 ; his spectacles, 15, 112

Tallien (Madame), 97

Tenby, Landor at, 67, 69, 75

Tennyson (Alfred, Lord), 204 ; ' Exhibition Ode,' 126 ; Landor and, 180, 181

Thackeray (William Makepeace), Landor and, 181, 182

Thiers (Louis Adolphe), 106, 268

Thorwaldsen (Albert), 19

Thuillier (General Sir H. Landor), 16, 20, 115

Tibullus, 54, 131

Tories, the, 143
Tribute, the, 180, 264
Turkey and the Armenians, 150
Twisleton (Hon. E.), 6, 257

Utrecht, Peace of, 140

Vespucci (Countess), 107
Vidocq, 106
Villari (Professor), 'Savonarola and his Times,' 26
Virgil and Horace, Imaginary Conversation, 121, 276
Virgil, compared with Ovid, 59
Voltaire, 101

Walker (Dr. Arthur de Noé), 2, 17 ; Landor's first meeting with,
114 ; verses to, 217 ; Landor's letters to, 115-129
Walpole (Horace), 123, 124
Walton's ' Compleat Angler,' 53
Washington (George), 208
Whateley (Archbishop), 123
Whigs and Tories, 143
Widcombe, 124, 198
William I. (King of Prussia), 206, 207
Wilson (Sir Robert), 250
Wiseman (Cardinal), 148, 271
Wordsworth (William), 63 ; ' Inscriptions in a Hermit's Cell,' 159 ; ' Laodamia,' 156 ; Landor and, 155 ; Landor's parody on, 158 ; the Waverley Novels and, 161

THE END.

BILLING AND SONS, PRINTERS, GUILDFORD.